WHITE TRASH *Damaged*

"Continues the sweet and poignant love story between Cass and Tucker. The new struggle feels realistic as Cass tries to adapt to life on the road with her rock-star boyfriend. . . . Fans will be thoroughly pleased with the epilogue."

—*RT Book Reviews*

"An emotional story that tugged on my heart strings. The story flowed seamlessly and beautifully from each page."

—*A Bookish Escape*

"I devoured it cover to cover!"

—*SMI BookClub*

WHITE TRASH *Beautiful*

"A fresh take on the Cinderella fairy tale. . . . Fans of the rock star genre will want to give this one a go, as this Prince Charming is a hot, tattooed musician. . . . Readers will meander through the dark and dangerous tunnel of Cass's life and, subsequently, cheer her on when she comes out the other side."

—*RT Book Reviews*

"An incredibly moving story . . . I felt like I was right there with Cass. You feel all her emotions to the point where you're connecting with her so much, you feel like you are her. [Mummert's] best book to date!"

—*New York Times* bestselling author Molly McAdams

"Enthralling . . . I felt a strong pull to Cass from the first line in the book . . . an emotional roller coaster that I never wanted to get off of. I couldn't put this book down."

—Amanda Bennett, author of *Time to Let Go*

"I loved it! . . . This story is filled with heartache and hope. Heartache for circumstance and life in general, but hope for a future."

—*Romantic Reading Escapes*

"It took exactly a few pages to realize I had no hope of pulling away. . . . I listened to my heart and devoured this novel."

—RebeccaBerto.com

"I loved this book. . . . Mummert put a lot of depth and soul into her characters."

—*Contagious Reads*

"I was HOOKED on this book. *White Trash Beautiful* is a gripping, emotional, and surprising tale."

—*My Book Addiction*

"Dark, edgy, emotional . . . I didn't want it to end!"

—*Belle's Book Bag*

"An emotional story full of hope, love, fear, and despair. . . . The romance was sweet and earnest. . . . I was burning through the pages. . . . Teresa Mummert is a wonderful writer."

—*Fictional Candy*

"*White Trash Beautiful* is the first book I have read by Teresa Mummert, but it is definitely not my last! I loved every minute of it even though parts of it broke my heart. . . . Just writing this review makes me want to read the book again."

—*Smardy Pants Book Blog*

Also in the WHITE TRASH Series
by Teresa Mummert

White Trash Beautiful

White Trash Damaged

A SONG

for Us

Teresa Mummert

G

GALLERY BOOKS

New York   London   Toronto   Sydney   New Delhi

G

Gallery Books
A Division of Simon & Schuster, Inc.
1230 Avenue of the Americas
New York, NY 10020

First Gallery Books trade paperback edition April 2014

GALLERY BOOKS and colophon are registered trademarks of Simon & Schuster, Inc.

For information about special discounts for bulk purchases, please contact Simon & Schuster Special Sales at 1-866-506-1949 or business@simonandschuster.com.

The Simon & Schuster Speakers Bureau can bring authors to your live event. For more information or to book an event, contact the Simon & Schuster Speakers Bureau at 1-866-248-3049 or visit our website at www.simonspeakers.com.

Interior design by Davina Mock-Maniscalco

Manufactured in the United States of America

10   9   8   7   6   5   4   3   2   1

Library of Congress Cataloging-in-Publication Data is available.

ISBN 978-1-4767-3209-1
ISBN 978-1-4767-3211-4 (ebook)

Thank you to all of the readers who took Cass and Tucker's journey with me. A special thanks to my husband and children. You've spent many hours without me in order for me to follow my dreams. I wouldn't have written a word if not for your encouragement and support.

A SONG

for Us

Prologue

I DIDN'T DESERVE TO be here but would gladly do it all over again.

I squeezed the dark bars in front of me until my knuckles turned white and my palms threatened to bleed, layers of paint chipping and sticking to my damp palms. The minutes felt like hours and my skin began to crawl with the waiting. I wasn't a bad person and sure as shit wasn't cut out to be locked in this shit hole. I've always heard that before you seek revenge you should dig two graves. This was mine. A place where I was locked away with my own thoughts that threatened to drive me insane. A place where I was forced to watch life pass me by and all I had were memories to cling to.

The walls were a deep gray that matched the floor. The only furniture was a metal bed attached to the wall and a toilet. Everything felt dirty and layered in grime. It was sickening.

Things weren't supposed to turn out this way. I should have been able to control my rage, but a man can only take so much.

CHAPTER
One

ERIC

Five Days Earlier

I'M NOT WEARING a fucking tie, Tuck," I growled as I tried to knot the silky fabric around my neck. I yanked it off and tossed it to the ground in frustration.

"You just need to learn how to tie it, Eric." Cass smiled as she patted me on the shoulder. "You would look good all dressed up."

I rolled my eyes and picked up the light blue scrap of fabric from the ground, determined to figure out how to wear it. Tucker laughed and shook his head. I owed it to Cass to try to be on my best behavior. She went through hell to plan this wedding around our schedule, and I wouldn't screw that up for her. We stayed in Southern California after our last gig, and she went to work ironing out the details with only two weeks until we go back to work. Each of us had his own job to do. I chose the church. It was small but sort of quaint, and the pastor talked my ear off for an hour about young love. I knew he wouldn't judge their decision to marry young.

"How come you listen to her and not me?"

"Because Cass is prettier than you," I joked, and Tucker rolled his eyes. "Seriously, why can't we just dress the way we always do? You want to start off your marriage with a lie?"

Cass's hand connected with the back of my head.

"Oww!" I yelled, then rubbed the tender spot. I knew she was stressed out about the ceremony, and it was too hard to resist messing with her. She had been trying her hardest to get Dorris to attend, but her health was failing and Cass finally gave up two days ago. I held out hope some of our friends would show, but it had been months since I'd talked to Sarah and I assumed Filth was touring and didn't have the time.

"You're not going to dress as a homeless rock star at my wedding," Cass called over her shoulder as she made her way to the hotel bathroom.

"I am a homeless rock star."

"Semantics," she called out with a laugh.

I was happy to be a rolling stone. Cass and Tuck had been talking about getting a home of their own, and the idea made me cringe. I didn't want things to change. I ran my hand through my hair and pushed out a sigh. Maybe the shots of Jack before lunch were a mistake. Drinking never took away my problems, but ever since our tour ended and Sarah—the girl who had gradually become my rock—was long gone, I didn't want to cope with reality.

It was easier to find peace at the bottom of a bottle.

"You all right?" Tucker asked, leaning in toward me and lowering his voice. His hand clamped on my shoulder. I knocked it away and took a step back from him.

"I'm fine."

The truth was, I was far from okay. I just didn't want to talk about it. I wanted to play another gig and get lost in the music.

I glanced up at Donna, our manager. Her dark, wavy hair was pinned back, but loose curls spilled down the back of her neck. I wanted to wrap my fingers in it. I shook the thought from my head and made my way to the kitchen area of our hotel suite. Donna had been loosening up around all of us a lot more lately—it was a refreshing change from the all-business bitch who first showed up to whip our band into shape during our tour. Sometimes we'd even flirt a little. And in the months since Sarah left, Donna and I had actually grown closer as friends. Plus, she was hot when she let herself kick back and have fun.

But I couldn't let my mind go there, especially not today . . .

Maybe the problem wasn't that I had drank; maybe I just didn't drink enough. I poured two fingers of whiskey into a glass and quickly drank it down, letting it burn my throat.

I sat the plastic cup on the counter and wiped a drop of liquor from my chin as Cass came to my side.

"I could use a few of those myself," she said quietly as she leaned her back against the faux-granite countertop.

I stared at the cabinets in front of me as I clenched my jaw. I knew Cass could tell I was upset. She had become like a little sister to me, and as much as I loved her, at times I wished we could escape each other. I hated how transparent I was to her, and she never let shit go.

"Have you talked to her?" I asked after a pregnant pause. Even thinking about her made my head start to ache, and I knew it was only a matter of time before I had one of my headaches.

Cass nodded, swallowing audibly.

"She doin' okay?"

"She . . . she said she is happy."

I could hear the pain in her voice and I closed my eyes, not wanting to see the look of pity on her face. It wasn't long ago I had judged Cass and Tucker, afraid of their ripping apart our band with their relationship. But now here I was, sad and sulking over someone I had no right to miss, not even wanting to think about how lost I'd be without Cass's and Tuck's support.

The conversation came to an abrupt halt when a hand slid over my spine. Even though I'd been doing my best to avoid Donna's most deliberate advances knowing it would only end badly for all of us, suddenly the idea of having someone touch me, distract me from my pain, even for a few hours, was all I wanted. And I wanted it more than anything else. I watched Tucker and the twins from the small kitchen area, trying not to meet her gaze. I didn't mind sometimes blurring the lines a little, but today was different. Today I was forced to watch others move on in their lives, build a future, and I was still lost and alone.

"You mind sharing?" Donna cocked an eyebrow at Cass, and I knew she wasn't talking about the alcohol. I rolled my eyes and Cass gave me a sympathetic smile.

"I need to go fix my hair. I'll talk to you later." Cass tucked a dirty-blond curl behind her ear and headed off to the bathroom of the hotel room. It was cramped with all of us in one room getting ready, but it was downtown and had a great view of the city. Donna insisted on letting us live a few days in luxury, even if she couldn't land us all rooms with personal hot tubs. We each had our own room, but after the wedding Cass and Tuck would be across town to get some privacy.

I slowly turned to look at Donna, who was wearing a low-cut, navy-blue dress that stopped midthigh and left little to the imagination. She smirked knowingly as my eyes finally landed on hers.

I poured her a shot into my glass and slid it across the dark faux-granite counter to her. She picked it up and raised it over her head to me before throwing it back. She scrunched her nose at the harshness of the liquor as she slammed the cup on the counter.

"Good shit, huh?" I laughed as she nodded, unable to speak. "Not much of a drinker?"

"Not yet. Pour me another."

"What's up with you today? Not a fan of weddings either?"

She shook her head, and her gaze dropped to the bottle. I nodded and poured her another shot, giving her a little extra this time. I slid the glass over to her again and she took it, her fingers sliding over mine. The electricity between us was undeniable today and I tensed, hating my attraction to her. She wasn't my type. She wasn't anyone's type. She was closed off and angry at the world. She used her work as an escape from living her life and enjoying herself. I also knew that any attraction she felt toward me was purely physical. Which wouldn't be a bad thing, except that she was our manager. I had to keep reminding myself of that.

"Wanna talk about it?"

She drank the shot, a trail of whiskey running over her chin and down her throat. I grabbed a paper towel and wiped it off for her, careful not to mess up her makeup.

"Just brings back bad memories."

I nodded, completely understanding. Even as Donna and I had grown closer over the past few weeks, I knew there were things she wouldn't tell even me. But I guess that was only fair, given how much I kept to myself, too.

"That's life," I said as I poured myself another drink. "A series of struggles strung together with the occasional moment of joy that makes it worth going another day." I turned around. Drink in hand as I looked over at Tucker. He was nervous but smiling in his charcoal-gray suit. Chris and Terry laughing and helping him shake his nerves.

"You think he is happy?" she asked as she leaned back against the counter, her body brushing against mine.

I cleared my throat and moved over a fraction of an inch. "Of course he is. Look at him. He's in love." I smiled, genuinely happy for my best friend.

"The deeper your love, the harder you fall when it goes bad."

I grinned, glancing over at Donna's profile; for twenty-seven she could really be intense. "Careful . . . you're dangerously close to opening up to someone."

She laughed sardonically and shook her head as she looked down at her shoes. "I won't make that mistake twice." She gave me a sideways glance, and the corner of her lips curled up in a small smile.

I didn't want to push her to say anything more, so I just offered a halfhearted smile in return. "I'll drink to that." I poured the amber liquid down my throat and tossed my glass in the sink behind us.

Donna grabbed the light blue tie from the counter and wrapped it around my neck. She was standing so close I could feel the heat radiating from her and the faint smell of her minty, alcohol-laced breath.

"You'll drink to anything." Her eyes narrowed as she worked quickly to secure the tie and fold my shirt collar down over it, her fingers lingering on my shoulders. My body moved on its own as I leaned forward a fraction of an inch, as if a magnet were pulling me toward her, or maybe I had drunk a few too many shots. I was thankful when Cass returned, her hair swept back at her nape. She was still wearing an old T-shirt and shorts.

"How you feeling?" she asked as her eyes danced between Donna and me.

Donna took a step back, looking embarrassed. "I'm going to freshen up." She left us and Cass smiled widely. We watched Donna walk away.

"She really has a thing for you."

"Nah. She just wants a distraction."

"You could both use one."

"Cass, you know I can't do that. There isn't anything there. The last thing I want to do is mess things up for the band over some chick."

Cass raised an eyebrow and I realized that probably sounded like an insult to her.

"You know I didn't mean you. You're like family to all of us."

"I wasn't always. I remember what it felt like to be an outsider in this group. Maybe Donna just needs to find her place."

"Donna is one of us, she just doesn't realize it."

Cass sighed loudly as she looked around the room. Her face looked sullen as her eyes glassed over.

"What is it?" I reached out and took her hand. She glanced down at the ring on her finger and shook her head, fighting back the tears.

"My dad."

"Hey . . ." I pulled her against me and wrapped my arms around her neck, giving her a nice firm hug. "We talked about this. You don't need him. I'm going to walk you down the aisle with the twins. You have all the family you need."

"I know."

I pulled back from her and ran my thumbs carefully under her eyes to catch the tears that began to spill over. She jerked back and made a gagging sound.

"Jesus, E! You smell like a bum! How much have you had?"

"Not nearly enough."

She smiled. "I could use a little relaxing myself. I can't stop shaking."

"You scared?"

"No, I'm not scared. I'm happy. I can't believe it is finally happening. It's overwhelming."

"What are you women talking 'bout?" Terry asked as he made his way into the cramped kitchen space and threw his arm over my shoulder. I pushed it off and took a step away from him.

"Just because I am sensitive to the ladies doesn't make me a chick."

"Doesn't make you much of a man either." Terry laughed.

"How much have you drunk, Terry?" Cass asked. He just laughed, his eyes glazed over and bloodshot.

"What does make you a man, O wise one?" I asked as Chris made his way to us.

"This," Terry shot back as he grabbed his crotch.

"A small package?" I joked, and glanced over at Chris.

"Let it be known we are fraternal, not identical," Chris replied as he winked at Cass, who let out a giggle.

"Thanks for the backup, Brother." Terry ran his hand through his hair and cracked his neck. Chris just shrugged and took a swig of his bottle of beer.

"Beatfest is in a few days," Chris said to no one in particular.

"Great. I wonder which one of you will get in a fight first at the festival." Cass rolled her eyes and shook her head.

"They all promised to behave," Tucker spoke up in our defense.

"They know how hard it was to convince you to stay here longer just for a concert."

"You still owe me one," she replied with an eyebrow raised.

"Oh, I will give you one tonight." He winked at her.

Chris made a heaving sound. "Seriously. That is gross. Cass is like a little sister to the rest of us."

"This is fun, guys, but you all need to get out so I can put on my dress. It's bad luck for Tucker to see me in it before the wedding."

"Fine, but I'm taking my whiskey with me," I smirked as I grabbed the bottle and headed for the hotel door.

The rest of the band followed, but Donna stayed behind to help Cass get ready. They didn't always see eye to eye, but Cass was lucky to have another female around for times like this.

The band all filed into the elevator and waited for it to make it to the expansive lobby. The doors popped open and a blinding flash caught us all off guard.

"Don't you have a fucking life?" I put my hand out to block the photographer's lens as Tucker and the guys hustled by to get to the waiting car outside.

Ever since we had performed at the MTV Music Video Awards about four months ago, we'd begun attracting more attention, especially from the paps. Most days we could go about our daily business freely and without interruption, but ever since word got out that Tucker had proposed, paparazzi had been counting down the days until he tied the knot, stalking us with obnoxious persistence.

Tucker has been pretty laid-back about it, but I couldn't keep my cool as easily.

"Don't touch my camera, man. I'll call the cops!"

"You're stalking us and you're gonna call the cops on *me*? Bitch move, man." I hurried after the guys and slid into the back of the murdered-out Escalade. The windows were tinted so black that even with the camera flash they couldn't get a decent shot of us. I flipped off the photog from behind my window as we pulled out into the street and headed toward the chapel.

"Thanks, man." Tucker nodded in my direction.

I smiled as I relaxed against the seat and stretched out my legs. "Not a problem."

"You should have let us throw you a bachelor party. It's bad luck not to see some tatas before your big day," Chris called out, causing the driver to glance in his rearview mirror at us.

"I don't want to go see some washed-up old lady swing around on a pole. I have the chick I want."

"Very noble of you, man, but I'd like to see some old naked chicks swing on a pole. Think of your friends, dude," Terry joked, and we all laughed.

"I told you we can do it in a few days . . . as long as Cass can come along."

"Why would you want to subject yourself to that?" Terry asked.

"She's going to be my wife."

"Could you imagine Donna in a strip club?" I laughed and shook my head as I tried to picture her uptight ass sitting in front of the stage. Even the more loosened-up version of Donna that seemed to be sticking around these days didn't fit in with that scene.

"It looks like you are imagining it, pervert." Chris laughed and hit me on the arm.

"Fuck off, man. It's not like that."

The car slowed to a stop when we reached the church, and Tucker took a deep breath as we all stared at him.

A large smile spread across his face. "I'm not gonna change my mind, guys. Let's do this."

The driver pulled open the door and we all exited. He had parked out back, and thankfully no assholes with cameras were there to greet us. Given how stressed out I was this morning, this was a good thing. I didn't need to be arrested for assault and miss the wedding of my best friend.

We filed inside the small, dimly lit building. It looked more like a post office than a church. I was shocked it didn't burst into flames as I entered. The priest greeted us as we walked in. He pulled Tucker to the side so they could speak privately and pointed to a room off to the left that we could wait in. We had ordered snacks and beverages to be ready for us while we waited, and they were lined up on a small card table against the wall. I still had my bottle of Jack, which I held down at my side so the preacher couldn't see it. I knew it was some-times part of religious ritual to drink wine in church, but I wasn't sure how they felt about something a little harder.

The holding room had a few foldout chairs and old paintings of Jesus on the cross. I wasn't a religious person, but I could certainly understand why so many people are. Knowing someone else was looking out for you and would have your back was comforting. But that didn't work for me. My thoughts always drifted to my little brother, and as hard as I tried, I couldn't understand where God was on the day he had died.

I unscrewed the lid to my bottle and took a healthy sip. The liquid no longer burned. My body was growing numb to its effects.

Terry walked up beside me, his hands folded over his chest as he nodded his chin toward the old oil painting. "Whatchya thinking about?" he asked, his eyes dipping down to the bottle in my hand before he looked back to the picture.

"Life . . . death . . . shit." My words were beginning to slur and I knew it was time to cut myself off. I didn't want to forget this day with Cass and Tucker.

"That's deep, man." Terry reached down and took the bottle from me with a grin on his face. "I think we should slow down a bit."

After a long pause he rubbed his hand hard over his freshly shaved chin as if deep in thought. "You ever wonder what Donna looks like naked?"

I shook my head and walked away, mumbling expletives under my breath. The guys were constantly ragging on me about Donna ever since they'd plotted to set us up a few months ago. They thought a game of pool and a few drinks would make me forget that Sarah was right next to me, and that she was back with that scumbag Derek, a jerk that didn't even come close to deserving a woman like her. I was thankful they did though, because that had been the turning point for me and Donna—when she'd started loosening up and opening up with me a little. I grabbed a bag of pretzels from Chris and shoved my hand in to grab a few. He yanked the bag back out of my hand with a laugh.

The door swung open and Tucker stepped inside, glancing behind him before letting the door close.

"You look like you saw a ghost," I joked as I shoved a pretzel in my mouth.

"I sort of did." He ran his hand over his hair, causing it to stick up haphazardly.

"You didn't see Cass in her dress, did you? That chick will flip the fuck out if you pull some bad-luck shit like that."

"No, not Cass. You know she invited some old friends to come. She didn't mention it because she didn't think they would be able to make it with their crazy schedule."

I pushed him aside as I pulled open the door and glanced out of the crack to the pews. My heart stopped as my eyes landed on Sarah. She was wearing a baby-blue dress to match the color scheme of the wedding. I rarely ever saw her in anything besides black, and it took my breath away. She looked beautiful, a softer side of her—one that people rarely got to see—shining through. I almost didn't see Derek at her side, his hand on her lower back, dangerously close to grabbing her ass. *Dick*.

Tucker pulled me back and the door shut again in front of my eyes. I squeezed them closed, wishing I hadn't drunk so many shots.

"It's fine," I lied with a smile as I threw my hands in the air. "So I thought she was cute. No big deal. You could have told me she was coming."

Chris shook his head and glanced over at Terry.

"For fuck's sake, guys. I'm not a lovesick puppy. I could give a fuck about Sarah and her shitty boyfriend. We're just friends. *Were* friends. Whatever, it was never anything more than that."

"All right, man." Tucker shrugged and forced a smile. "I'm glad to hear it."

I clenched my jaw and closed my eyes, taking in a deep, calming breath. I wasn't going to let some chick fuck with my head. Not today. Cass and Tucker didn't need my pointless drama. Sarah was smiling and didn't seem the least bit fazed by the contact between her and Derek. She was . . . happy. I was going to do my best to pretend I was happy, too.

"I need some air." I pushed out of the door before anyone could stop me. I knew they thought I was going to make a scene, but I didn't care. I felt as if the walls were closing in on me, and that picture of Jesus staring at me was beginning to creep me out. It felt as if he were silently judging me as he hung on that wall . . . on that cross.

I didn't glance Sarah and Derek's way as I stepped out of the front doors of the church and pulled my cigarettes and lighter from my pocket. I didn't realize my mistake before it was too late. I should have gone out the back. Instead, I was face-to-face with the same asshole photographer from the hotel lobby. He grinned as he raised his camera to his face and snapped a pic.

I lit my cigarette, desperately trying to bite my tongue. The door opened behind me and Sarah stepped out next to me. The tightening in my chest was painful, and trying to convince myself, once again, that she was just a friend—if that anymore—was nearly impossible. I wanted to reach out and touch her smooth skin, wrap my arms around her, and bury my face in her hair, but she had stopped returning my texts or calls months ago without ever explaining why—though I could venture that it had something to do with Derek.

But I had no idea where our relationship stood anymore. The thought of her being able to dismiss me so easily was too much, and I pushed the idea away and focused on the cigarette that glowed hot in my hand. The photographer began to yell questions at us, asking if we were together.

"Long time no see." She sighed loudly as she stared off at the street.

I nodded, squinting in the bright sunlight. It was overbearingly warm out and my stomach began to turn from the alcohol. "How've you been?" I asked, still unable to look at her. It was no secret I had a thing for her, and if everyone else could see it, I knew she could, too.

"Can't complain."

"Can't or won't?" I finally chanced a glance at her and smiled when her eyes met mine. Sarah was forced to grow up fast the way I had, and it was one of the reasons we had become so close while on the road together. We were exposed to the ugly side of life when we should have been hanging out with friends and playing games.

Witnessing my brother's death when he was hit by a car had destroyed me. We stood in the front yard of our home as on any other day. I threw around a football with Robert, who was only nine at the time, but he wanted to be just like me when he got older. As I threw the ball, there was a screeching of tires and the entire world slowed to a stop as I spun around to see a light blue Buick careening toward us. I panicked, unable to inhale as my eyes darted back to my brother, who was still smiling, oblivious to what was about to happen. It was the most horrific day of my life. Everyone knew, but no one ever brought it up. Sarah did the complete opposite. She forced me to face it so I could start to move past it.

"Both I suppose."

"Get closer together!" the photog yelled at us.

"Get a real fucking job," I snapped back. His camera began to click faster as he continued to try to get a rise out of me.

"Don't let him get to you," Sarah said under her breath.

The door opened behind us and we both turned around to see Derek, his eyes darting back and forth between us before landing on Sarah. He ran his hand roughly through his dark, shoulder-length hair.

"Cass is here. She's asking for you."

"It was good talking to you, E." Her lips tugged up into a small grin as she stepped inside. I let the door close completely before I took another long drag from my cigarette and flicked it toward the photographer. He swore loudly as I opened the door to the church and slid inside, smiling from ear to ear.

My eyes flicked to the other door at the far end of the chapel that concealed the girls before I headed into the private room that held the band. I stopped as I stepped inside and Derek stood before me.

"What's up, man?" I asked casually as I made my way to the snack table and nonchalantly poured myself a Jack and Coke.

"Nothing really. Was just telling the guys about a concert we had a few weeks back outside of Vegas. It was wild, man. The chicks were insane." He was no longer talking to just me, and I gulped down my beverage, crumpling the plastic cup in my hand as he rambled on about some groupie who was willing to do anything to sneak off with him. Tucker placed his hand on my shoulder and I nodded at him, letting him know I was not going to fuck up this day for him. He patted my back before taking the bottle and pouring himself a drink.

"She made her choice. You can't do anything to help her if she doesn't want to be helped," he said quietly as the twins laughed loudly at something Derek had said. *She made her choice.* Those words stung like a motherfucker. I ran the back of my hand over my lips as I let that reality sink in.

It was time for me to make a choice and stop sitting around waiting for someone who didn't want me. It was just a fucking crush. I wasn't even sure if Sarah had ever felt the same way about me. We would flirt, sure, but it never went any further than that.

As if she were listening into my thoughts, the door popped open and Sarah stuck her head inside. "It's time." She grinned, her eyes meeting mine briefly before she looked down to the floor.

Tucker followed her out of the door, and after a few more words, so did Derek. I glanced at Terry, unable to hide the anger in my eyes, before stepping out of the room and following the others to Cass's room. All three of us would be walking her down the aisle in the absence of her father.

Cass looked incredible in a simple white gown that went all the way to the floor. She had insisted on this weird strappy shit that went across her back. I teased her for days about getting tangled in it, but she'd made the right choice. Her hair was pulled up in lose curls, and the only jewelry she wore was her engagement ring and that damn heart locket from Tuck that she never removed. I couldn't help but smile with pride as she beamed back at me, her makeup making her look as if she'd stepped off a runway. I knew she had learned to wear it that way from Sarah. We had butted heads when Cass first came to be a part of our dysfunctional little family, but I had grown to love her.

"She cleans up nice, doesn't she?" A voice broke through the silence and my eyes fell on Dorris. She was much thinner since the last time I had seen her, and she had aged at least ten years. Her lips curled up in a smile and I crossed the room in two large strides to hug her.

"It's been too long." I gave her an extra squeeze before she pulled back to look me over. "Does Tuck know you're here?"

"Not yet." Her smile grew. "I told him I wasn't able to fly."

"He's going to be excited. You were the one thing he said would be missing."

"That and a good meal. You boys are so thin." Her eyes danced over the twins, who came over to give her a hug. Terry lifted her from the ground and she squealed, smacking him on the shoulder so he would put her down. "Hasn't Cass been feeding you?"

"They eat like horses. I can hardly keep up," Cass joked, running her hand down the front of her silky dress.

"I'll have to send you some of my recipes. Tucker always loved my lasagna."

"I'd appreciate that. Thank you," Cass said.

CHAPTER

Two

SARAH

DAMAGED AND FILTH had become like family during our tour, and it was amazing to be back with them all. It was like coming home. My eyes drifted over Derek, who sat next to me on the pew. I wondered how it was possible for Cass and Tuck to maintain that "first love" mentality when only a few weeks after the tour ended Derek had already begun to grow distant again. Living on the road is stressful, and going from one gig to the next wears you down. I hoped this trip would help us relax. At the least, I knew that this time he was being faithful.

He looked bored as his foot jumped against the hardwood floor. He didn't believe in marriage and wouldn't even entertain the idea of making a bigger commitment. But I felt that he was all talk, that maybe he'd come around. We'd had some rough patches, but we always found our way back to each other—in a lot of ways, he'd become my rock, and it was getting harder and harder to imagine my life without him these days.

I placed my hand on his knee to still his movements. He flicked my arm and I jumped.

"Stop that! You know I hate when you do that."

I mumbled under my breath as I looked up at Tucker, who was standing in the front of the room, shifting his weight from foot to foot. He looked more excited than nervous, and it made me smile knowing Cass had found someone who truly loved her.

A lot had changed since we had gone on tour with Damaged. Our band was playing more gigs and that meant a lot of long hours on the road. It was nearly impossible to get a decent night's sleep, and on top of that, the partying intensified.

I envied Cass and Tucker for being able to walk through hell and back together and still smile when their eyes met. I glanced over at Derek and he winked at me, causing my heart to skip a beat. He was good at frustrating me one minute and melting my heart the next.

E stepped out of the door in the back of the room, and his eyes met mine briefly before he made his way to Tucker and whispered something quietly to him. Tucker grinned and said something back to him.

"I still don't like that asshole," Derek's angry voice broke through my thoughts.

"He's a good guy"—I cleared my throat—"and you know

he's been through a lot. What is your problem with him, anyway? He never did anything to you."

Derek's eyes met mine now. "Did he ever do anything to *you?*"

I hated that someone I had once considered one of my closest friends and my boyfriend didn't get along. Derek had always been jealous of the friendship I had developed with E when Derek and I had first split up. Two weeks after the tour ended, Derek and I had gotten into a huge fight because E had texted me in the middle of the night after having another meltdown, and since then Derek had forced me to cut off communication with E entirely. But that was just how E and I worked. He listened to me and let me talk him off a ledge when no one else could get through to him. Then I would ramble for hours about my own problems, and he would just listen until his breathing would even out and I knew he was back to sleep. It didn't mean we were sleeping together, it just meant we got each other, something that Derek had never been able to understand. Or maybe he just couldn't help but feel threatened by E, by the thought of our connecting in some way. Either way, Derek just couldn't seem to deal with it, not even now, after weeks of silence between E and me.

"No. He's just a friend."

"I see the way he looks at you. That guy's been eye-fucking you since we joined the tour. I still don't buy the 'just friends' garbage."

I sighed as I struggled to not let my frustration get the best of me. I had given up a great friendship for Derek, but he still wouldn't let it go. I knew his own infidelity in the past caused him to be concerned, but it was wasted emotion. I had never cheated on Derek, even in our darkest moments.

"It's never been like that with E."

"I trust you, Sarah. It's him that I don't trust." Derek ran his hand over his shoulder-length, black hair as he relaxed in his seat.

"Then you have nothing to worry about because I'm not going anywhere."

"You promised me."

I could only nod. I knew it would be impossible to maintain a friendship with E when he and my boyfriend hated each other. The door in the back of the room opened again and Dorris walked out, limping slightly. Tucker's face lit up and he ran to meet her at the end of the aisle. My eyes found Eric's and he was staring at me, his face hard. The intensity of his gaze made it impossible to look away. I was surprised to feel a fluttering in my stomach. Was he making me nervous?

He wasn't the angry asshole most thought he was. He had a deeper side to him that few got to see. Donna came out of the little room and made her way to E, saying something quietly to him. She wrapped her arms around his and led him back to the back of the church.

"I always thought he was tapping that." Derek laughed.

I rolled my eyes. The thought of E and Donna was laugh-able. He had told me a hundred times that he wouldn't risk their friendship—or her sometimes precarious position as the band's manager—for a one-night stand. If Derek only knew him the way I did, he'd know E just didn't chase hot women for the sake of getting laid. And he wouldn't ever hit on me, either.

Dorris, Damaged's former manager, took a seat on the other side of the church pews, and Tucker made his way back to the front to stand by the preacher. Soon after, Donna was sitting by Dorris's side, and the wedding was ready to begin. Music began to swell, signaling the bride's entrance. For a rocker couple's wedding, I was surprised that they'd gone with the traditional "Wedding March."

Cass looked stunning in her simple silk dress, with criss-cross backing. As usual, she didn't need to cover herself in jewelry and makeup. She was naturally beautiful. She kept it simple with a small necklace and a little bit of makeup to play up her features. The rest of the band walked by her side as she slowly made her way to Tucker, like magnets drawn to each other. The "Wedding March" continued to play quietly in the background, and Tucker's eyes grew wide and his lips quirked in a loving smile.

The love they had for each other radiated off them. I wondered if anyone ever looked at Derek and me and felt that way.

The ceremony was simple but perfect. Tucker and Cass didn't write their own vows beforehand, but spoke honestly from their hearts about their love for each other. I cried as they spoke, and Derek gave my hand a little squeeze. I smiled over at him. His face softened and his eyes filled with warmth. The hardness that usually defined his expression seemed to slip away, just for a moment, revealing that the old Derek who had stolen my heart all that time ago was still in there, even after all we had been through. Trying to maintain a committed relationship while living the rock-and-roll lifestyle is nearly impossible, but we had survived thus far.

"I can't wait until we are up there," I whispered, trying to gauge whether seeing Tucker and Cass making such a moving commitment to each other was having an impact on Derek's rocker bravado.

But Derek just looked over at me and rolled his eyes as he shook his head. "Sarah . . ."

"What? You can't blame me for trying," I grumbled. Derek had told me from day one he never planned to get married, but I still hoped he would change his mind, especially now that things had gotten so serious with us.

"We don't need a stupid piece of paper to show that we love each other. It's not important."

"It's not important to *you*, and if it is so stupid, why not just humor me?"

"You're killing me, woman."

After the ceremony everyone stood and made their way to the center of the room to congratulate the newlyweds. I hugged Cass and we both cried. Derek's arm went over my shoulders and he pulled me against his side, my hand falling to his chest.

"When are we hitting the strip club?" Derek asked, and my heart sank.

I looked up at E, whose gaze was locked on mine, causing me to squirm. I didn't remember his being so . . . intense.

"Come on, man. I want to spend tonight with my bride." Tucker laughed as he pulled Cass into his arms and kissed her on the forehead. "How long you in LA for?"

"We'll be here for two weeks."

My eyes danced around the plain church as memories of my past began to wash over me.

"Why do you have to marry him?" I asked my mother as she finished braiding my hair and securing a tie around the end.

"He's not a bad guy, Sarah Bear. He's good to me and to you kids."

"He's creepy." I folded my arms over my chest and my mother just laughed. I had no real reason to hate Phil. But sometimes his eyes lingered on me for just a second too long and his hugs seemed to be just a little too tight. I could feel it in my gut—something just wasn't right.

"I don't expect you to understand what love is. You're only eleven, but one day you will know what he means to me and maybe then you can be happy for me," she snapped, and I felt

like the world's biggest jerk. Now I had upset Mom on her big day.

"You've only been with him for four months. Why can't you just date him like a normal person?" I huffed.

She laughed as her hands smoothed over her cream-colored silk gown that stopped just below her knees. "Normal people get married."

"Yeah, well, he is a jerk, and he is always yelling at me like he's my dad or something." I wanted to tell her how uncomfortable he made me, but I knew she would just think I was trying to get them to break up. I wasn't exactly accepting of him from the first moment he walked into our lives. He moved in only three weeks after Mom introduced us to him. What if Dad came back? Our family would never be back together if Mom was with this guy.

"You're right, Sarah. He's not your dad. Your dad couldn't handle being a father and ran off with the neighbor."

"Maybe lightning will strike twice."

"You stop that right now!" Her voice was a low whisper and she was practically growling. "Your sister is only seven and she isn't acting like a brat. Why are you? You should be thankful someone even wants to join this family. It's not often a guy will take on someone else's kids."

I glanced over at my little sister; her hair was a shade lighter than mine and curled at the bottom. She was holding a bouquet of cream-colored flowers and pulling off the petals.

*"Stop it, you idiot. You're ruining her flowers!" I snapped,
and my sister frowned as tears formed in her eyes.*

*"Stop fighting with your sister, Sarah. Don't you take out
your childish anger on her."*

"You okay?" Cass asked.

It took a moment for her words to sink in and for the memories to be pushed aside. I nodded and forced a smile.

"You don't look happy." She frowned.

"I'm great. Weddings . . ." I rolled my eyes as I glanced around the group.

"Yeah, I get it." She was now beaming from ear to ear as her eyes fell on her new husband. She didn't get it and I was glad. I carefully placed my mask back in place. I wasn't going to let my memories ruin her big day.

"You look amazing," I whispered to her and she pulled me into her arms for a hug. I needed that hug more than she realized. She'd become like a sister to me on the road, and I had missed having her in my life so much these past few weeks. I couldn't even remember the last time I'd seen or heard from my own sister, and sometimes I felt that Derek and the guys were the only family I had left in the world.

CHAPTER

Three

ERIC

I PULLED MY TIE loose and fell against the inside of my hotel-room door. I felt as if I were suffocating. I had been trying to push what day it was out of my head for Cass and Tucker's sake, but I was missing my brother more than ever and it killed me to force a smile,

I hadn't realized how much I had missed Sarah until I looked into her eyes. She always seemed to see past the bullshit, as if she was looking at the real me. It scared the fuck out of me but it was also freeing. So why couldn't she see what kind of asshole Derek was? Why would she subject herself to his constant mind games and cheating?

I pinched the bridge of my nose as I struggled to fight off the headache that was slowly beginning to throb in my head. I just didn't want to see her get hurt. That is what I told myself. Denying my feelings was a hell of a lot less scary than accepting how much I liked her . . . and yet would never have her. It was always hard to never have a place I could call home. I felt that I was never where I was supposed to be. I was always just on the outside, watching everyone else being happy. It was like chasing a shadow. I could never get close enough without surrounding myself in darkness.

A tiny knock came from behind me and I shook my head as I pulled open the door to Donna, still wearing her low-cut dress with no shoes and a bottle of sparkling wine in her hand.

The small smile that played on her lips faded as she saw my face. "What's wrong?"

I stepped to the side so she could enter my room. "One of my headaches," I half lied as I made my way toward the bed, sitting down on the edge and cradling my head in my hands.

After a moment, I slowly looked up to see Donna still standing by the door. "What?" I stretched my neck from side to side, trying to relieve some of the pain.

"She's pretty. I get it, but you need to focus on the band."

It took a moment to understand what she was talking about. "Yeah, well, she is someone else's. If the guys sent you over here to talk me off a fucking ledge, I don't want to hear it. We're just friends."

Donna nodded, chewing on her lower lip as she looked down at her bare toes. Being off-duty during this hiatus from our tour seemed to be bringing out that softer, more relaxed side of her tonight. "No one sent me over here, E." She held up the bottle of wine as her eyes met mine and she smiled. She was really letting her guard down. "I was just trying to help and I figured you'd be up for a drink. I know I could use one and I don't feel like drinking alone."

"Why is that?" I relaxed back onto my elbows as she made her way across the room and sat down next to me. I knew that someone had broken her heart. She had slipped up once when she had too much to drink, started to tell me about her ex . . . but when she'd sobered up the next day, she pretended not to remember having opened up. I'd been trying to get it out of her ever since, but she always changed the subject. Which I got—so I never really pushed it.

But suddenly I wanted to know more.

She shrugged as she struggled to uncork the top to the bottle. I took it from her hands and popped it open, holding it out for her.

"I don't know." She shrugged again as she tipped the bottle to her lips and took a sip. A trail of bubbly liquid trickled down her chin and she struggled not to laugh and spill it everywhere. I took the bottle from her hands, pulling it slowly away from her wet lips, and took a drink. Her eyes watched my mouth as I titled the bottle up. Whatever her ex did, it had left her scared to get close to anyone, but I knew she craved it—closeness, intimacy—more than anything else.

"She is stupid if she doesn't see you are better than him."

I laughed sardonically as I shook my head. "I'm not exactly a prize."

"You don't give yourself enough credit." She bumped her shoulder against mine and laughed nervously.

"I guess that makes two of us."

"I'll drink to that." She took the bottle back, her delicate fingers sliding over mine as our eyes locked. There was no denying the attraction between Donna and me. We were cut from the same cloth. She just masked her pain with the illusion of perfection. I hid behind my anger. Same problem, different Band-Aid.

I watched her tilt the bottle to her lips, wrapping them around the rim, and I had to move away from her. I pushed to my feet and paced the floor as I scratched the back of my head. My hair had grown out in the last few weeks and now was a shaggy dirty-blond mess.

"I need to get out of here." I was beginning to feel like a caged animal in my own thoughts, and being alone with Donna was a regret waiting to happen. She needed this band as much as we needed her, and for that reason alone I was going to keep my hands to myself.

"All right. I'll head back to my room. I just wanted to make sure you were all right." She stood and took a step forward as I turned to continue my path across the room. Our bodies nearly collided and I put my hands up, grabbing her arms to keep us from crashing together.

"You're coming with me." I wasn't about to abandon a friend when he or she needed me because I was busy sulking over my own bullshit. Getting out would do us both some good, and I wasn't about to go hang out with the twins while that fucking asshole was around.

"Oh . . . all right, but I'm not bailing you out if you get in another fight. Just let me go change." My eyes scanned down her body; her dress revealed the top of her breasts and her breathing had grown heavy, pushing them toward me with every inhale.

"You look good. Just grab your shoes."

Her cheeks tinged pink as she smiled. I let my hands slide off her silky skin. I grabbed the bottle from her hand and sat it on the counter behind us. "We can finish that later. Let's go get something a little stronger."

As I opened the door to the hotel room, I placed my hand on the small of Donna's back to guide her out of the room. When I stepped into the brightly lit hall, my eyes locked with Sarah's as she swiped her key card in a room just three doors down.

Her mouth opened as if she was going to say something, but her door pulled open and she practically fell inside as I heard the sound of Derek's muffled voice. I swallowed hard as Donna and I walked in Sarah's direction.

As we passed the door, which still hung open, Derek glanced out at us and smiled. "You two are like a thing now, huh?"

I glanced over his shoulder to Sarah and back to him. "We're just hanging out."

"Whatever, man." He glanced back at Sarah behind him. "We're just getting ready to hit the bar scene with the twins. You guys should come. Would suck to be the only couple there."

I glanced to Donna, who shrugged but didn't want to commit to anything. I knew she was worried it would upset me more to be around Sarah, but Derek was holding out an olive branch and I would be stupid not to take it.

"Yeah, just let her grab some shoes. We'll meet you in the lobby." I pushed my fingertips against Donna's lower back and she began walking toward her room two doors down on the left. When we got inside, I slammed her door a little harder than necessary.

"Sorry about that," I sighed as she grabbed her shoes and slipped them on her feet.

"It's fine." Her tone had a bite as she ran her fingers through the loose curls that hung around her face.

"If you don't want to go, we can just hang out."

"I don't want you to be embarrassed when people think we are a couple."

"What?" I said. She tried to walk by me, but I grabbed her arm, stopping her beside me. "Why do you think I would be embarrassed?"

She sighed, her shoulders sagging as she looked at my chest, avoiding eye contact. "What does it matter if Derek and Sarah think we are a couple? Am I that much of an outcast? I know what you all think about me, but am I really that repulsive?"

I took my free hand and titled her chin up with my fingers. "It matters because we aren't, Donna. And none of us think you are repulsive. You're just a bitch." I laughed as I saw the familiar frustration roll over her face.

She knocked my hand away as her eyebrows pulled together. "I know we aren't. But why does it matter? If Derek thinks you aren't looking at Sarah, he won't care if you're around. And maybe Sarah seeing you with someone else will make her realize what she is missing."

I hadn't thought of that. I let go of Donna's arm as a smile spread across my face. "You're kind of evil," I joked. She grinned wickedly and winked at me. I wrapped my arm over her shoulder and pulled her head closer, kissing her on the forehead.

"I have my moments." She giggled as I pulled open the door to her room, and we made our way down to the lobby.

The twins were already waiting for us and they turned around, eyebrows rising as they saw me with my arm around Donna. The elevator next to us opened and Derek and Sarah stepped out.

"This is going to be fun," Chris said, laughing, and Terry shook his head. I just glanced at Donna, who smiled and slipped her arm behind my back.

"Where we hitting first?" Derek asked as we walked across the lobby toward the front door.

"I figured we'd hit a few bars and get a good buzz on before we find a club," Terry called over his shoulder as we stepped out into the cool night.

I walked behind Sarah and Derek, getting a view of his hand grabbing her ass. I clenched my jaw and swallowed back the jealousy just as her hand swept behind her and knocked his away. I couldn't help but grin a little bit at her clear annoyance.

Then he reached over and flicked her ribs and she glared at him. I could tell it really bothered her, but Derek was a clueless fucking idiot. Clearly he thought he was being playful or something. He just didn't get her at all.

I laughed and Donna looked up at me through her thick, dark lashes. I just shook my head as we walked down the sidewalk toward a large neon sign ahead.

CHAPTER Four

SARAH

I WASN'T SURPRISED THAT E was with someone, but I didn't expect it to be his manager. She didn't seem like his type. Even though she was around our age and seemed cool enough, she was definitely more uptight and professional than E, and E was just . . . E.

Derek seemed to relax a little when he discovered they were together, and that made me feel a little more at ease. I didn't want this trip to be ruined by his perpetual bad mood over my past with E. Derek just didn't believe that we'd only ever been friends. Unfortunately, that was a side effect of his own cheating, even if it was way in the past—he just never trusted anyone anymore. But I knew that dealing with his insecurities was part of dating Derek—it just came with the territory.

But still, if he wasn't worried about E, we could all hang out, and that is all I wanted. I missed Damaged. Life on the road without those guys—and Cass, especially—had been a lot more stressful. Our band just didn't mesh the way theirs did, especially with all the drama between Derek and me lately.

We slipped inside the Wet Room, just a few blocks from our hotel. I was so glad we had an entire two weeks to relax and hang with our friends before getting back on the road. I loved the stage, but we *all* needed some time to relax.

The thumping music pulsed through my body and drowned out any lingering thoughts of E. Derek slipped his hand in mine, pulling me behind him, as we navigated our way through the crowded bar. I wasn't much of a hand-holder, but I was happy not to get lost in the throngs of people stuffed into the room. The bar had to be at capacity and it was nearly impossible to move.

We found a booth along the right wall, and Donna and I slid in as the guys went to order us a round. We stared out at the crowd of dancing bodies as the lights flashed red and blue over them. The lack of conversation would have been awkward if not for the loud music.

"It's nice to get out of the hotel for a little bit," Donna yelled to be heard.

I nodded and smiled as the image of her and E locked away in a hotel flashed in my mind. They had separate rooms and I wanted to ask her why that was, but it wasn't my place. I didn't know Donna well.

"So, you and E . . ." My voice trailed off.

She stared out at the crowd. "He's a good guy."

"Jesus, this place is fucking crazy," Terry yelled as he reached the booth. Donna slid over closer to me in the half-oval bench seat so he could sit. E showed up with two drinks in hand as he looked down at me.

"Oh, sorry!" I slid out of the booth so he could slide in beside Donna. I stood at the edge of the table awkwardly for a moment before I sat back down, keeping space between E and me. E handed a drink to Donna and leaned closer to her ear to say something, and I wondered what they were talking about.

"Where's Derek?" I yelled.

E turned to look at me before scanning the crowd and shrugging. "I think he went to the bathroom." He slid his mixed drink in front of me. "Here. You can have mine while you wait."

"Thank you." I smiled over at him and my eyes fell to the hand that was resting on his leg. Donna's hand. I picked up the drink and took a sip as I pondered their relationship. They didn't seem like a good fit for each other, but E seemed happier than I remembered.

Chris came back and, without saying a word, slid in next to me, bumping my hip and shoving me closer to E until my side was pressed against his.

"Sorry!"

He turned his head toward me and our noses nearly touched. "What?" he mouthed, and leaned closer so my head was next to his ear.

The smell of his polo sport washed over me. "I said I was sorry."

He pulled back to look at me, his brow furrowed, before placing his lips next to my ear. "You don't ever need to apologize for touching me." As he pulled back, he winked and turned to resume his conversation with Terry on the other side of the table. Such a notorious flirt. I shook my head—I swear he only did things like that to mess with Derek.

I grabbed my drink and sucked down half of it. My throat burned. It was practically straight liquor with just a splash of soda.

"I should go look for Derek," I said to Chris, who was nursing a beer on the other side of me. He glanced down at me and back to his beer as he set it on the table.

"I'm sure he is just stuck in line at the bathroom." His gaze flicked to Terry and there was some silent exchange.

I rolled my eyes. I hated when they communicated in code like that. "Whatever, just let me out, Chris." E looked to Chris and nodded. Chris sighed and slid out of the booth so I could get out, just as Derek showed up at the table.

"Hey, this place is crazy, man." Derek's eyes were already glossed over, and he slipped in front of Chris and tapped my thigh for me to slide back into the booth. I did, pushing my leg flush against E's as Chris squeezed in on the end.

"Where were you?" I asked as Derek ran his hand over his mouth.

"I was getting a fucking drink. This is a bar."

"Where is mine?"

He laughed as he shook his head. "I may have drank it." He smiled as he looked over at me, the smell of vodka on his breath. "What's yours is mine, right? Or some such shit like that."

"Fuck you." I rolled my eyes as I laughed.

"Oh?" He cocked his head to the side and lowered his voice. "Right now?"

I felt Eric's body stiffen beside me as his shoulder pressed harder against mine. "There's ladies here, man," he said loud enough for Derek to hear.

"I must have missed them." Derek laughed again but there was no humor, and I knew he was trying to start a fight.

E didn't take the bait. He shrugged as he grabbed Donna's drink and drank it down. He leaned over so his lips brushed against the shell of my ear. "I won't fight with him. You can relax."

E always had the reputation of flying off the handle, but he wasn't a bad guy and was actually a lot kinder than most in our business. Still, the endless fights after our gigs had earned him a reputation that wasn't easy to shake. He was always the first one to shove a photog, freak out at an overzealous groupie, or even flip out at one of us if he thought the set didn't go well. He just had a short fuse, and he seemed to be almost always on edge, especially lately.

I glanced over at him and his gaze didn't waver. I knew he would keep his temper in check for the sake of our friendship.

"Who needs another round?" Chris asked, and we all held up a hand. "I'm going to need some extra hands. Help me out, buddy?" He stood and looked down at Derek. Derek nodded and slid out of the booth. I breathed a sigh of relief that he would have a few minutes to cool off.

"So . . ." Terry ran his hand through his dark hair with a smirk on his face. "He's kind of a dick still."

E laughed.

I narrowed my eyes at him. "He's just stressed. We all are."

"I'll drink to that," E said, and Donna laughed, laying her head on his shoulder.

"Maybe I should go back to the room. I'm not really feeling up to this."

"You're a rock star. Partying is in your blood," Terry yelled.

"I'm just the boobs of this operation," I joked, and rolled my eyes. E's deep laugh shook his whole body against my side and he turned, flashing me a smile, revealing a deep dimple in his cheek. I couldn't help but smile back at him.

"Why don't we dance?" Donna grinned up at E, her bottom lip between her teeth.

My heart sank a little when he nodded in agreement. I didn't want to be left in the booth alone. Terry slid out of the seat, and Donna and E followed him. As they began to walk off, E turned back to me and held out his hand.

"You coming?"

I looked around for any sight of Derek and Chris, but they were nowhere to be found.

"What have you got to lose?" E asked.

"My street cred," I joked as I slid out of my seat and put my hand in his before I could second-guess my decision.

I thought he would drop my hand as I rose to my feet, but instead he curled his fingers around mine and pulled me in the direction that Donna and Terry had gone. His thumb ran softly over my knuckles as we navigated through the dancers.

Donna was dancing in front of Terry, who was already receiving attention from other women. I began to sway my hips to the beat of the booming base.

"I couldn't find you!" Derek called from behind me, and E's head snapped in that direction as his fingers slipped from mine. Derek lifted a cup over my shoulder for me to take.

"Thanks," I yelled back as he put his free hand on my hip and pressed his body against me from behind. His hips began to move with mine as I quickly downed my shot.

Chris handed out the shots to the others, and they yelled cheers as they all tipped their heads back and drank. E only glanced over at Derek and me for a second before he pulled

Donna against him and began to dance. She smiled as she looped her arms around his neck, her right leg between his legs as they moved against each other. E's hands moved down her back as he whispered something in her ear, and she shook her head as her fingers went into his hair and she gazed up into his eyes. The moment suddenly seemed intimate and private, so I quickly looked away, feeling invasive.

Derek's hands ran over my hip bones as he held me against him. "I'm sorry I was such an asshole." His lips found my neck and I let my eyes flutter closed as I melted against his rock-solid chest. I knew he was trying, and that was all I could ask for from him. He had always dreamed of being a star, and having a girlfriend on your hip definitely wasn't a part of that plan, but we'd fallen quickly and we'd fallen hard. The rest was rock-and-roll history.

"I forgive you," I sighed as he nipped the base of my neck with his teeth.

"You're too good to me."

CHAPTER

Five

ERIC

I DON'T KNOW WHAT I was thinking by inviting her out to dance. I knew I would never be able to get close enough to even touch her, but as she'd put her hand in mine, I couldn't bring myself to let go. I would have been happy standing there all night surrounded by hundreds of strangers if she would stand with me.

Of course, like death and taxes, Derek was unavoidable.

As I saw him come up behind her, I had to fight the urge to pull her against me. Instead, I let her fingers slide from mine as he pressed his body into hers.

A smile spread across her face as she whirled around and her body melted into his on the dance floor. His hand drifted down to her ass, but instead of swatting it away, she let it linger there, clearly just losing herself in the music, in the moment, in him.

During the tour, Sarah and I had spent hours together, just talking and talking, revealing so many of our secrets . . . but I never had the guts to tell her how I really felt about her. But now I'm glad I held that truth back because Derek is the one who gets to hold her in his arms.

She made her choice.

The words vibrated throughout my soul and I wanted to call him out on everything. What she knew about his bad behavior paled in comparison to what I had seen him do. None of it mattered because she clearly loved him enough to put up with it. I tried to tell myself that if this made her happy, I had no right to tell her what I was feeling. It wasn't fair for her . . . but this wasn't fair to me either.

Part of me wanted to leave so I could spend the evening alone with the pain in my chest and a bottle of Jack, but I looked to Donna, her hair falling lose and hanging wildly around her face. Her skin was glistening with sweat from all of the people in such a small space. She looked incredible . . . but more important, she looked like the perfect distraction.

I reached out and grabbed her wrists, pulling her body against mine. Her hands landed on my chest as we began to move against each other. She smiled up at me, her lips parted as her arms looped around my neck. My hand began to slide down her back as my body reacted to her touch.

"If you want me to stop . . . ," I whispered in her ear, and she shook her head as her fingers slid into my hair. The pressure in my chest began to ease as I let go and focused on Donna. When we were on tour, she could be so guarded. I knew she had a rough past, that her "all-business" attitude was just a front, protection, and I'd only just begun to get a sense of the real Donna. But when she had a few drinks in her, she relaxed and showed a side of her few got to see. This was one of the reasons we had become such close friends over the past few months. The fear of commitment that had kept her at arm's length melted away.

"You know what I love about you?" She was smiling, fears forgotten.

"What?" I couldn't help but grin at her now-playful forwardness. I loved when she let this side of her show.

"Everything. I know I'm not the easiest person to get along with. Thank you for giving me a chance." Her smile fell and my breath caught at her admission. My own grin faded as I looked into her eyes, the truth reflecting back at me. She put on a front to keep people away, but I knew she needed someone just like the rest of us. Her eyes fell and I put my fingers under her chin to tilt her head back up so her eyes could meet mine.

"You can talk to me, Donna."

"Just dance with me."

We danced through half a dozen songs as the twins continued to grab rounds from the bar. By the seventh shot my vision had blurred enough that I no longer needed to glance over at Sarah, because I couldn't see her.

Donna grinding her ass against me definitely helped. She smelled like expensive perfume that you find samples of in those chick magazines. I wondered briefly if she tasted as good as she smelled.

My hands ran up her sides, pulling and tugging at the delicate fabric of her dress. She turned back around to face me, her breasts pressed against my chest, and I knew she could feel how much I enjoyed it as I held her waist against mine. Her forehead was against mine as our noses touched, and my gaze fell from her eyes to her lips. Suddenly, I heard Sarah laugh, and my eyes darted over to her and Derek. Even with Donna in my arms, my mind flooded with images of Sarah. What would it be like to take Sarah in my arms and run my hands over her, to have her nails drag through my hair, to drag my tongue over her soft lips?

In that moment I knew I was going to do something I would later regret. I needed to push Sarah further out of my mind, and Donna suddenly felt like the only way to do that. She needed me as an escape just as much as I needed her.

Donna's tongue ran out over her lips, and every rational thought I had disappeared as my mouth crushed against hers. She moaned quietly against my kiss as I sucked her lower lip between mine, grazing it with my teeth. My hands slipped onto her ass as I ran my tongue over the seam of her lips. She let them fall open, inviting me in.

She tasted even better than I had imagined. Her lips tasted like strawberries from her gloss and the ghost of the last shot she had drunk. Her hands slid down the sides of my neck and her nails bit into my shoulders as we struggled to get even closer to each other.

The bass of the music faded in and out, and I could only hear my own heartbeat thudding in my ears as her tongue pushed back against mine. In the distance I heard someone yell, but I blocked it out as my hand ran over Donna's ribs, my thumb grazing the bottom of her breast.

I know I'll regret this later on. I know that anything involving Donna is complicated given her role in the band. I know I am not thinking clearly, but in this moment, all I want is for someone else to want me. No, I want someone else to crave me. I'm tired of sitting on the sideline while the asshole gets the girl. I want the girl.

"E," Donna moaned into my mouth, and melted my remaining willpower.

Suddenly, someone crashed into us and I stumbled, clinging to Donna to keep her on her feet. I glanced around at the crowd with hazy vision, struggling to focus on the swarm of bodies around us. A man with full sleeves of dark ink was yelling at another guy for groping his girlfriend, who was nowhere in sight, and the crowd grew hot and cracked with palpable tension. You could taste it in the air. Alcohol and lowered inhibitions craved something more—chaos was about to break out.

Before I could make my way out of the crowd, arms were flying and people were being shoved against one another. I wrapped my arm instinctively around Donna and tried to work my way through the fight. I had to shove and kick people out of the way, but I got her back to our table. Chris was on his feet and ready to push his way into the brawl.

I took a minute to steady my breathing before I looked around and panic set in.

"Where's Sarah?" I yelled, and no one responded. "Where's

Sarah?" I yelled louder, and Donna jumped at the tone of my voice. I peeled her from my side and sat her down in the booth as I placed my face directly in front of hers. She looks to be in shock and I wanted to make sure she took in everything I said.

"Don't move from this spot. I will come back for you. Don't move."

"Don't go back out there." I heard the fear in her voice. I don't know if she was scared to be alone or for my safety.

"Don't move, Donna. I'll come back. I promise." She nodded and I stood up, glancing over at Chris. A worried look was all over his face as the fight grew out of control, but I couldn't leave Sarah in the middle of this. I knew Derek wasn't putting her safety above his. He never put her first.

The screams were deafening as we worked our way back into the fight. Women were fighting and getting knocked to the ground as men exchanged blows. Chris shoved people out of our way and I grabbed some asshole by the back collar of his shirt and pulled him to the ground. I stepped over him as I moved forward in the crowd.

My heart stopped as I saw Sarah. Her hair was wild and black streaks stained her face from crying in her makeup. She looked absolutely terrified and lost as chaos erupted around us, with Derek nowhere in sight. I reach my hand out to her and she hesitated to take it as her eyes widened and she screamed my name. I didn't have time to react as an elbow connected with my temple. The shooting pain was excruciating, bringing on one of my migraines that makes it impossible for me to think. I fell to a knee and stumbled as I pushed back to my feet. I held out my hand again to Sarah as several bodies pushed in between us. Her fingertips brushed against mine, sending a jolt of electricity through me. I had never before seen her so frightened.

"Grab my hand." I yelled over the noise.

She pulled back, pushing herself against the bar. "I'm scared!"

"Trust me, Sarah. Take my hand." Her fingers slid in mine and I pulled her between the other people and against my chest. She curled into me, so fragile and scared.

"I thought everyone left me." She sobbed and I held her tighter.

"I wouldn't leave you, Sarah."

"I couldn't find any of you."

I clenched my jaw as I wondered where Derek was and why he hadn't kept her safe. I nodded to Chris, who now had Terry by his side. They started to clear a path and guide us back to the table where I'd left Donna.

She pushed up from her seat and wrapped her arms around my neck as Sarah stepped out of the way. My eyes fell on hers wishing I could hold her and comfort her, but it wasn't my place. I rubbed my hand over Donna's back as I whispered in her hair that everything would be all right, but I couldn't take my eyes off Sarah's sad face.

"I didn't think you'd make it back in one piece," Donna whispered against my neck, and I swallowed hard, knowing our friendship was going to suffer from tonight.

"Me either."

I watched as her throat moved and she swallowed hard, fresh tears in her eyes.

"We need to get the fuck out of here. Cops are coming," Terry yelled, and I nodded to him, tucking Donna against my side as he put an arm around Sarah. Chris pushed a way through the crowd to the door and we followed behind. Sarah stopped as we reached the exit, her face turning to mine as she struggled against Terry's grip on her.

"We can't leave Derek."

"The fuck we can't." Terry pulled her back against him and stepped out into the cool night air. She twisted in his grip, her eyes pleading and begging for me to help her. I had no choice.

"Go with Chris and Terry. They will make sure you get back safe, okay?" I tried to keep my tone light as I talked to Donna. She looked petrified, but I didn't want her to keep me any longer. I needed to get in and out of the club before the police showed, and I could already hear the faint sounds of sirens in the distance.

"You can't go back in there." She shook her head.

I brushed the hair back from her face, running the pad of my finger down her cheek. "I'll be fine. I promise." I nodded. "Do you trust me?" She hesitated, knowing she could answer honestly and let me go or she could lie. She slowly nodded and I grabbed the sides of her face in my hands and pulled her toward me to kiss her forehead.

"Take them back to the hotel," I barked at Chris as I headed back into the club.

Terry leaned in close to me with a stern look on his face. "He ain't worth it."

My eyes flicked to Sarah's. "She is." I turned and made my way back into the club before I could hear any more protests. My head throbbed from the blow to my temple and I had to steady myself to keep from doubling over. I knew I had to find Derek because she needed me to, but I couldn't promise I wouldn't kick his ass when I finally saw him.

My eyes scanned the club and it was impossible to see who was who. I pushed my way into the mess, catching a blow to the ribs and having to swing against some asshole. I caught him under the jaw and shoved him back into a group of men behind him, who yelled like wild animals.

It took me a full five minutes to reach the bar, but it felt like hours and I knew I would be too sore to even move tomorrow. I pulled myself up onto the bar and looked down at the people below. It was a tangled sea of limbs. I couldn't find Derek anywhere in the mess and I was about to give up, but I didn't want to disappoint Sarah.

I looked behind me to an open doorway that led to another room. I jumped down and fought my way over to the hidden space. The fight had spilled over into the doorway, but the majority of occupants were bystanders huddled around pool tables and watching as all hell broke loose.

That was when I saw him. And I saw red. Derek was leaning against a wall with some dumb blond bitch pressed against his body and his tongue in her mouth. He was oblivious of my presence, but he wouldn't be for long. I shoved out of the way some asshole that squared his shoulders, looking for a fight. When I reached Derek, I didn't hesitate to grab the slut's shoulder and pull her back while I swung with my right arm and my fist connected with his left cheekbone. The crack of knuckles against bone was only mildly satisfying as I drew back to hit him again, but someone grabbed my arm and I was pulled backward and stumbled to the ground, my blood pumping so hard I nearly blacked out from the pain in my head.

"He's not worth it. We need to get the fuck out of here." Terry held out his hand for me and I took it, blinking back the pain that radiated through my head.

CHAPTER
Six

SARAH

*I*PACED THE FLOOR of my hotel room playing nervously with my silver chain necklace as I waited for E to return with Derek.

When a knock came at the door, I rushed to open it, and Eric stood in front of me, blood spattered on his lip. He looked as if he had just run a marathon.

"Where's Derek?" I asked as he ran his hand over his face and stepped inside the room. I closed the door behind him and hurried into the small kitchenette to get him a drink of water.

He gulped it down, looking pained as he tried to swallow. "I need something . . . for my head."

I rushed over to my purse and dug through it, looking for

anything that might ease his migraine. "Fuck, E, I can't find anything."

"I have something in my room." He took an unsteady step toward the door and I rushed to his side, grabbing his arm to help him. "I'll walk you." He only nodded as I pulled the door open and we slipped down the hall toward his room. He glanced over his shoulder toward Donna's room as Terry stood outside it, ready to knock. He tilted his chin up to E, who nodded as I pulled him to his room.

"I need your room key."

E patted down his pockets but his hands flew up to his head as his face contorted in pain.

"I'll . . . I'll get it." I hesitated before slipping my hand in his front right pocket, coming up with a lighter. His eyes opened, locking onto mine. I held my breath as I pulled my hand back and stuck it in his other pocket and pulled out the plastic card.

I slid it in the card slot, and the little green indicator light flashed and then I pushed down the handle and shoved the door open. E leaned against my side and I wrapped my arm around his lean, muscular waist and guided him inside until we stood at the foot of his bed. He groaned and fell back onto it and stared up at the ceiling.

I scanned the room. "Where are your pills?"

He pointed in no particular direction and I took off into the bathroom.

A label-less orange medicine bottle sat on the edge of the sink. I tried three times with shaky fingers before removing the childproof lid and grabbing him one of his pills.

When I made it back to him, he was shirtless and my gaze immediately fell to his thick chest and the rippled muscles of his abdomen. He was unbuckling his dark jeans and my eyes slowly slid back up his body and locked onto his. I was embarrassed he had caught me staring, and he smirked knowingly as he shoved his pants over his hips.

"I . . . I found the pills." I held out my hand to show him, and he sank down on the bed in only a pair of black boxer briefs. I tried to look anywhere but at him as I made my way over and extended my arm.

"Thank you." His voice was rough and low as he popped the pill in his mouth and swallowed.

"I should have gotten you a drink."

He shook his head, his eyes closed as he fell onto his back. "It's fine. I take them dry all the time."

I was wringing my hands together as I watched his chest rise and fall. I forced my eyes not to venture any lower. My heart rate was finally beginning to settle to a normal rhythm after my worry for him. Then my mind froze as I realized that in my worry for Eric, I had forgotten Derek.

"E?"

He didn't respond.

"Eric?"

"Mmm?" His eyebrow rose but he kept his eyes closed.

"Where is Derek?"

I watched his Adam's apple jump as he swallowed. "Why do you put up with that asshole?"

"What kind of question is that? E, tell me where he is."

He slowly turned his head toward me and blinked his eyes open as he searched my face. I could tell he was struggling to find the words, and my heart sank as I imagined the worst.

"Why does he get to fuck up and I have to be the one to break your heart?"

"Please, just tell me, E. Please. You're scaring me."

He shook his head and looked up to the ceiling above him. "The cops came right after you guys left. I was able to get out of the club, but they arrested Derek for fighting." E squeezed his eyes closed and took a deep breath. "He was trying to find you to make sure you were safe."

My hand went absentmindedly to my chest as my heart broke for Derek.

"How do I get him out, E? Where do I go?"

"He will be released in the morning. You'll have him back in no time . . . I'm sorry."

"No, don't be sorry. You tried to find him . . . thank you."

He nodded but didn't reply.

I stood by his bedside for a moment as I wondered what Derek was going through. "Is there anything I can do to make you feel better?"

He looked over at me with a grin and shook his head. "No." I turned to leave the room, but as I got to the door, his voice stopped me.

"It would have been his birthday today."

My heart broke as I realized he was talking about his little brother.

"Can you hang out for a bit? Just talk to me while I fall asleep?" I turned around to face him. He was still lying on his back, his legs over the edge of the bed. One arm was over his forehead to block the light, and the other was stretched out to his side in my direction. "It will help keep my mind focused on something else, something good . . . drown out the darkness, you know?"

If I went back to my room, I would only spend the night pacing the floor and worrying about Derek. There was nothing wrong with my spending time with E. He was my friend and he proved he was Derek's by going back for him at the club.

I slowly walked back toward the bed, kicking off my heels as I moved alongside it and sat on the edge above E. "What do you want to talk about?" I slid back farther and lay slowly onto my back so our bodies formed a *T* on the bed.

"Anything. Just want to listen to your voice."

I sighed as my fingers looped in my necklace and I twisted around my pointer finger. "Are you sure you don't want me to get Donna?"

"No. She had a lot to drink. I'm sure she is asleep by now or she would have come over."

"How long have the two of you been together?"

"It just sort of happened." He groaned.

"She doesn't seem like your type." I studied the tiles on the ceiling.

"I don't have a type."

"Everyone has a type."

He rolled over and put his fists under his chin so he was looking up at me, and I realized how close our faces were. "What's your type?"

I focused on counting the holes in the tiles, not wanting to turn and look him in the eye. My heart was racing as I lay so close to him while he was practically naked. I felt like a whore for even being in here while Derek sat in jail because he wanted to save me. It wasn't like him, and it gave me hope that he and I might be able to work past our problems.

"I dunno." I shrugged as I pulled my lip between my teeth, biting down.

"Everyone has a type," he mocked me.

I rolled my eyes and sighed as I continued to tug on my necklace. "I like rockers, of course. Anyone who loves music. It's important to me, ya know?"

"I do," he said quietly as I snuck a glance over to him. Having his arms bent the way he did made his muscles in his arms bulge, and I'd never realized how built he was.

"I like someone who is considerate and kind. Puts others before themselves."

"That doesn't sound like Derek."

"You don't know him like I do."

"Fair enough." He shrugged and rolled back onto his back. I was thankful he was no longer staring at me.

"Fair is fair. I told you my type, now you tell me yours."

"If we played by those rules, why am I the only one who is nearly naked?" He laughed quietly, vibrating the bed.

"You're avoiding my question." I don't know why I cared.

"I told you. I don't have a type." I rolled my eyes but he continued, "There's just a person. She gets me. I've never met anyone like her, and I know she is the one I'm supposed to be with."

I was surprised by how much his words stung. Maybe it was hearing him talk about Donna the way I sometimes wished Derek would talk about me. I knew that, in his heart, Derek did love me, and I knew we were good together, maybe even great. But seeing the expression on Eric's face—that look of genuine emotion—made my heart ache. I had loved Derek from the moment I met him. He was the life of the party and everyone wanted to be his friend. It only took two days for us to realize we should be together. Our relationship had always been a crazy kind of love. We fought and hurt each other, but we could never stay away. About a year ago Derek had taken things a step too far and cheated on me with a groupie. I found out when his cell phone had accidentally dialed mine while he was in the act. We split up after that, even though we still were in the same band. It was hard to watch him move on with life without me, and I realized that I didn't want him to. We vowed never to hurt each other again, and now we were in it for the long haul.

Donna was lucky to have someone such as Eric, someone who so clearly adored her. I thought of how safe I felt the moment Eric found me during the fight. How Donna had clung to him as we made our way outside. How he risked his own safety to go back inside for Derek because I asked him to. I was starting to feel sick as my thoughts swirled. I shook the thoughts from my mind. I was just exhausted, and coming off a night of way too much booze.

"Where'd you go, just now?" His voice cut through my thoughts and I struggled to come up with something to say. Suddenly I just needed to get out, clear my head.

"Derek would be mad that I am in here," I blurted out as I sat up.

E's fingers wrapped around my wrist and I was terrified he would feel how frantic my pulse became as he touched me. His fingers slid over the raised scars across my arm as he looked over my tattoo, the word ROCK. I had gotten it almost a year ago now, to remind me of Derek. And to cover the etches in my skin, a piece of my past that I wanted to forget.

"You mention this to your mother and I'll start paying your sister visits. You think you can keep a secret, Sarah?" Phil ran

his hand through his sandy hair. He looked like the perfect businessman, but I could see the evil in his eyes from the first day I had met him.

"I won't say anything." I wiped a tear from my cheek as I struggled to block out what had just happened.

"That's a good girl." He kissed me on the forehead and I wanted to scrub my face with bleach as I waited for him to slip out of my room, leaving me alone in the darkness. Sobs ripped through my chest as I slid off my bed and onto my knees on the hard wooden floor. I reached under my bed, feeling for the small wooden keepsake box. I sighed, relieved as my fingers landed on the box, and I pulled it out, holding it against my chest.

I slowly lifted the lid and grabbed the old razor that my father had left behind when he ran off with his girlfriend two years before.

It was an old plastic disposable. Nothing special about it, but it belonged to him and that made it invaluable. It hurt when he had left us behind. It hurt that I had to endure Phil because of him. All of the pain needed an outlet, and as I dragged the old blade across the inside of my arm, I released it all. All of my anger and sadness slipped out in long, red streaks, dripping onto the wooden floor below.

Part of me was ashamed of what I was doing, and part of me was crying out for someone else to see the hurt that I kept buried inside.

I wanted to pull away from him, embarrassed, but E wasn't looking at me with pity. He wasn't judging me, but he was also not ignoring it the way Derek always did. Suddenly I felt that we were right back in our tour bus, just talking and swapping life stories, and it was comforting.

"I won't say anything."

My gaze dropped to E's hand and then went back to his eyes.

"This is what friends do, Sarah. They hang out and talk to each other. I missed that about us."

I pulled my arms around myself and swallowed hard.

"I don't think Donna would be happy." I also knew that Derek would be pissed if he spent the night in jail while I was hanging out with E.

"What would make *you* happy?"

My eyes snapped up to meet his, and I was suddenly terrified by the intensity of his gaze. I pushed to my feet. I always felt that E could see straight past my bullshit as no one else could. He could sense the secrets that I hid from everyone else. Secrets I was too ashamed to even share with my boyfriend.

"It's been good seeing you again, E." I took a step backward toward the door, and he pushed to his feet.

"But?" He stepped forward and I instinctively took another step back.

"But I didn't want to cause any problems for you. You seem . . . happy."

"But you're not." He stepped again and I did the same.

"I am." My voice was weak, my mask slipping. "I know you don't like Derek, but he has changed. He and I are planning a future together."

E shook his head, running his hand over his messy hair. It had grown out since I had last seen him, and he looked as if he belonged on the cover of a magazine more than on a stage behind a drum kit.

CHAPTER

Seven

ERIC

THE DESIRE TO be closer to Sarah drowned out the throbbing of my head. She was running from me, but I could see in her eyes she had felt something. Even if she didn't, I hated that she was with that fucking asshole. I could have helped put the final nail in that coffin tonight, but I couldn't bring myself to look her in the eye and tell her he was cheating on her again. It would have killed her, and I wouldn't be any kind of a man if I let her run into my arms while she ran from his.

I wanted her to want me as badly as I wanted her. And what I was going through with Sarah was gutting me. But Sarah had never been mine. Our relationship had never gone further than friendly flirting. And I had to remind myself that it never would.

I stepped forward, pulled toward Sarah. "I just want you to stay."

She took one final step backward as she leaned against the door.

"I can't. Sleep it off, E." Her words were barely a whisper, and her eyes were pleading with me. Her hand felt for the door handle next to her waist and she grabbed ahold of it. I reached out, wrapping my fingers around hers, leaning closer. Her chest was rising and falling quickly, her lips parted. I looked down at her mouth and her tongue darted out, running over her lips. I could barely control my own breathing and I struggled not to press myself against her. I needed to feel her skin against mine. I glanced down at her baby-blue dress as my forehead pushed against hers and our breaths mingled.

Her eyes fell closed and I stared down at her thick lashes, getting high from her proximity. "Please," I whispered, and her free hand came up to press against my chest. She weakly pushed back against me, her nails biting into my flesh. I'd grown painfully hard and I wanted to push my hips against hers, but I stayed inches away as she held me back.

Her eyes slowly opened and she searched mine. "You're drunk, E. Knock it off."

"Sarah . . ." My words caught in my throat as I stared down at her.

Without thinking, I pressed my mouth hard against hers. Her lips moved against mine for a brief second before she shoved against my chest hard, causing me to stumble back a step.

"What the hell is wrong with you?" she yelled as her eyes narrowed and her cheeks flamed red.

Her hand slid from my chest and she pushed down the handle to the door. Her eyes stayed on mine as she pulled it open and slipped out into the hallway.

The stabbing pain in my head came back full force as she walked out the door. I stumbled back to my bed and collapsed on top of the covers. I had taken a chance. I had put my feelings out there and she said no. I traced the spot on my chest that still burned from her touch.

It felt as if someone had cracked open my ribs and pulled my heart from my chest. Someone who cheated on her and degraded her was more appealing than me.

I wanted to go down to the police station and finish beating the piss out of Derek, but it wasn't my place. Sarah loved him, not me, and I had no right to interfere with her life anymore.

I forced myself to keep my eyes open for hours. Every time I tried to fall asleep, all I saw was her sad face. Eventually, my eyes grew heavy and burned and I had to give in to my exhaustion.

MORNING CAME TOO early and my throat was painfully dry. I made my way into the bathroom, groaning as I turned on the light. My eyes fell on the mirror and I took in the damage from the night before. My lip was swollen and busted and a small bruise was on my temple, but otherwise all of my pain was inside.

I tried to block out the foggy memories from last night, hoping the alcohol would help to erase them, but they all came rushing back. I turned on the faucet and splashed cold water on my face, wincing as it burned my cut. I cupped my hands and drank a sip, relieving the burn in my throat.

Leaning against the sink, I forced myself to think of something other than Sarah. I grabbed my bottle of pain pills and took one as I wondered how Tuck and Cass were doing. I was tempted to call Cass and tell her how badly I had fucked up again last night, but I didn't want to disturb the little bit of time they had alone.

Instead, I ran through the shower and pulled on fresh clothes, a pair of worn jeans and a white T-shirt. I grabbed my cell phone and looked at the time. It was already afternoon. I dialed Donna's phone, hoping she would be awake.

She answered after two rings, sounding as if she had been up for hours. "I didn't think you were going to grace us with your presence today."

"Yeah . . . ," I groaned, and stretched. "I feel like total shit."

"Nothing a little greasy food won't cure. I'm down at Hembrough's Diner. You want me to bring you something?"

"Nah . . . I'll come meet you. I need to get out of this fucking place."

"See you soon."

I said good-bye and hung up the phone, tossing it on the bed. I slipped on my sneakers and grabbed my cigarettes and wallet, and my eyes fell on a pair of high heels next to the bed. Just fucking great. I grabbed them and slipped out of my room, not ready to face Sarah after last night. I had made a complete fucking fool of myself.

I slowed as I made my way toward Sarah's door, taking a deep breath and knocking before I could talk myself out of it. I knew I needed to apologize. I couldn't just avoid her like an asshole and pretend nothing happened.

She pulled it open, just peeking her head out of a crack. "What are you doing here?" Her voice was a whisper, laced with anger, and she glanced back over her shoulder. I clenched my jaw when I realized that Derek must be inside. I could only imagine how fucked-up his face was this morning, and I braced for her to scream at me for hurting him.

I held up her shoes between us and she rolled her eyes, snatching them from my hand and tossing them on the floor inside the door.

"How is he?" I asked, feigning concern.

"He's passed out. He didn't sleep for shit in jail and his face is battered and bruised." She folded her arms over her chest. "I can't believe he went through that for me."

Shock was the first emotion that rolled through me, followed by the desire to shove my way in his room and beat his ass again. "Yeah, he's a fucking saint."

"Shhh . . ." She pushed lightly against my chest and I took a step back as she slid into the hall and pulled the door closed behind her. My gaze dropped to her hand on my body, and every emotion I felt last night when I was so close to her came rushing back to the surface. She must have felt it, too, and she quickly pulled her arm back, wringing her hands together.

"I never said Derek was perfect, but he is trying. Last night is proof of that. You do remember last night, don't you?" Her eyes narrowed angrily.

I rolled my eyes, wanting to scream that he wasn't changing and that I was the one who had battered his face, but I knew she would just hate me for that, so I kept my mouth shut and swallowed back the truth yet again. If I couldn't be with Sarah, I needed to save our friendship. I couldn't handle losing her altogether.

"I'm sorry for last night, Sarah. I should never have put you in that position. I had way too much to drink and I acted like an asshole."

Her gaze avoided mine as she listened to my half-assed apology.

"Still friends?" I asked, forcing a smile.

"Always." She returned the smile and we looked at each other for a long moment before my phone began to ring in my pocket. I pulled it out and looked at the screen.

"It's Donna. I gotta go."

Sarah only nodded and opened the door to her room. I watched her slip inside before making my way down the hall to the elevator.

CHAPTER Eight

SARAH

I CLOSED THE DOOR to the hotel room quietly and leaned back against it. My heart sank into my stomach as I stared at Derek, sprawled on the bed. All I could think about all night was E. Why did he have to complicate our friendship? It had felt so good to start to reconnect with him, to move past the awkward radio silence that had defined the last few weeks between us, but then he had to go and do something that he *knew* would piss me off, not to mention Derek.

My mind was racing; I was pissed and confused.

And why did it suddenly piss me off that he was going to meet up with Donna? I banged my head against the door as if I were trying to knock some clarity into my mind, and the sound seemed to bring Derek back to life.

"What's up?" Derek groaned as he stretched across the bed.

"Nothing. I just don't feel well. I think I drank too much last night."

He laughed and patted a spot next to him on the bed. I pushed to my feet and slowly made my way over to him. His one eye was completely swollen shut, his cheekbone bruised and split open.

I sat down next to him and ran my fingertips over his cheek. "They got you good."

He rolled over and wrapped his arms around my waist. "Yeah, but I won." He let out a low laugh and coughed.

"Let me get you some water." I went to stand but Derek's grip tightened around my waist, holding me next to him.

"I'm fine. I just need some more sleep. Have you seen any of the guys?"

My heart began to race as I thought of what to say. Derek had been right about E, and telling him that would only cause a fight. "Not since last night. E went back in the club to look for you for me, but the cops came before he could find you."

Derek smiled and nodded his head. "I'll have to thank him later."

I smiled down at him, glad that maybe he and E might finally be able to put some of their differences behind them and be friends.

"Come here." He pulled me down so I was lying with my back to him as he snuggled against me. "Wake me up in an hour." He yawned and laid his head against my back. I tried to relax against him, but I felt as if everything had changed in just a few short hours. It was killing me inside. Derek was finally trying. He was coming around and doing the right thing, but all I could think about was E. I closed my eyes as a tear slid onto the sheet below and prayed that sleep would take away my guilt, even if just for an hour.

WHEN I FINALLY woke, I didn't feel any better. I wished I had someone I could talk to, but E was definitely not a good choice and Cass was still off celebrating her marriage. I felt so alone, even with my boyfriend's arms locked around my body. I glanced at the alarm clock next to the bed. It was almost dinnertime and I had slept a lot longer than I intended. I pulled Derek's arm off me and slowly slid out of bed to use the bathroom. I knew I should wake him, but I needed a few more minutes to myself.

I ran a hot bath and slid into the tub, my hair piled on top of my head with a clip. I wanted to disappear underneath the bubbles so I didn't have to face the world again. I closed my eyes, getting lost in the warmth.

"Why didn't you wake me?" Derek's voice startled me.

I jumped, splashing water over the edge of the tub. I tried not to let the fear from memories of my past show on my face. "You looked so peaceful. I figured you could use a little more sleep."

He lifted the lid to the toilet and peed.

I gave him a look of disgust as I pushed myself up and grabbed a towel, wrapping it around myself. The bubbles still clung to my skin, but I needed to get out of there. The room was closing in on me. Derek zipped up his pants and grabbed my arm as I tried to walk by him and out the door. His nose skimmed along my jawline up to my ear.

"I know how you could make me feel better." His teeth nipped gently on my earlobe, and his hand trailed down my arm and gripped the towel in his hand, pulling it from my body and letting it fall to the floor. "It killed me not being here with you last night."

He turned toward me, lacing his hands behind my neck and pulling my mouth to his, reminding me of what had drawn us together in the first place—that magnetic pull that was impossible to deny. Those strong arms that had always made me feel so protected.

Derek's kisses were hungry and he grabbed his shirt, pulling it over his head and dropping it on the towel. My eyes danced over his tattooed chest before he pulled me back against him, needing to feel his skin on mine. His palm ran roughly over my breast as his lips moved over my jaw and down my throat.

The memories of kissing E flooded me, and my head began to swim with regret as I pushed against his chest to get away from his touch. I wasn't feeling guilty for keeping it a secret. I felt guilty because I'd liked it.

"What's gotten into you?"

"Nothing. I just want to take it slow." I pressed my lips against his, desperate to ignite the fire that had nearly flickered out. Derek backed me up against the bathroom wall, his body slamming hard against mine as he undid his pants and shoved them down his hips. Slow wasn't an option and I squeezed my eyes closed, hoping he couldn't feel how fast my heart was racing. I begged my brain to focus on the now.

The opening notes to "Free Bird" began to play in my mind, and I focused on the song as I let my mind detach from my body. I'd never enjoyed sex, but how do you explain that to your boyfriend? How do you even begin to tell the rock god you're dating that you don't feel like making love?

The lyrics grew louder in my subconscious as I let my imagination wander. Unfortunately, it went to the one thought I wished I could forget: kissing E.

CHAPTER
Nine

ERIC

COULDN'T GET MY mind off Sarah as I spun a beer bottle in my
hand.

"Shit, you've got it fucking bad." Chris laughed and took a drink
from his bottle as he motioned for the bartender to bring another round.

"I don't know what you're talking about."

"The fuck you don't, man. You nearly killed Derek last night."

"I was being a good friend. You would have done the same."

"Maybe. But I would have told her what he did. Why wouldn't you
dime him out? She would have ran right into your arms."

"Because I want her to *want* me, not settle for me."

"That's fucking deep. You're starting to sound like Tuck."

"That's what scares me."

The bartender brought our drinks and I picked mine up. Nodding to Chris, I slowly nursed it. "She won't leave him. She thinks he's changed." I stared ahead at the half-empty bottles of beer.

"She say that?"

I nodded, hating how my chest tightened when I thought of her.

"What does Donna think about all this?"

"She knows we are just friends. We're just having some fun."

"Like when you nearly fucked her on the dance floor last night? You're treading in dangerous territory, man. Women don't ever just want to be friends with benefits. They catch feelings faster than my brother gets STDs."

I chuckled and shook my head as Chris pulled his phone from his pocket and typed out a message.

"What's up?"

"Letting Terry know where we're at."

I grabbed my phone from my pocket and sent a text to Donna so she could come out with Terry and not have to walk alone. After we'd had a late lunch at the diner, she went back to her room to get some work done and set up dates and locations for our next tour.

Chris leaned over my shoulder to read my message.

"Get the fuck out of here, man." I used my elbow to block him from reading over my shoulder.

"I can't wait to watch this train wreck."

TERRY SHOWED UP at the bar an hour later with Donna, who was wearing tight jeans and a black tank top that read DAMAGED across her chest. Unfortunately, he also brought Sarah and Derek. I downed the rest of my beer and ordered another as I prepared for a fight. I wasn't sure Derek was stupid enough to say who fucked up his face just to keep me from Sarah, but he had been known to make worse decisions.

The bar was smaller than the club we hit last night, but just as crowded. Donna sat on my knee and I looped my arm loosely around her waist as I absentmindedly pulled at a loose thread on the thigh of her jeans. I owed her big-time for playing the perfect girlfriend role, although I'm sure she was enjoying being included in the group. It had to be miserable always pushing everyone away.

Derek sat on the other side of Chris, and Sarah stood between his legs with her back resting against his chest. Her dark gray skirt only came down midthigh, and it was hard not to stare at her long legs.

I swallowed down my feelings so I could prove to her that we could just be friends. I wasn't going to risk losing her over some stupid fucking crush.

"What the fuck happened to your face?" Chris called over to Derek, knowing damn well I was what happened.

"Fight was intense last night." Derek looked around Chris to me. "I heard you came to find me. Good looking out, man."

"It's no big deal. I would do it again," I smirked, and Terry laughed from behind me.

"Looks like it hurts," Terry called out.

Derek shook his head with a laugh before his eyes locked on

mine. "Sarah kissed it and made it better." He pressed his lips against her cheek, and my skin felt as if it were on fire.

My eyes went to Sarah's but she was looking down at the ground now and her cheeks were reddening as they had last night after I had kissed her.

Donna pulled at my arm that I had tightened around her waist to get me to relax so she could breathe. She leaned back, placing her lips next to my ear.

"If you snap me in half, I am going to demand a raise," she whispered, and I laughed, turning to make a face at her, our lips nearly touching.

"I'm sorry," I whispered back as I tried not to let Derek get to me.

"If he gets you to fight him in front of her, he wins, and I'm stuck trying to get you out of jail."

"He already won. I won't go after someone who doesn't want me."

Donna smiled sadly and nodded as she took my drink from my hand and took a sip. "Does this mean I need to find my own barstool?"

I gave her a small squeeze, holding her in place. "I'd be offended if you did. How much rejection can one man's ego take?"

Inside, every piece of me felt fractured, but I smiled for the sake of saving my friendship. If Sarah needed to know I wasn't going to pursue her, I would show her, even if it killed me inside to do it.

I placed a soft kiss on Donna's cheek and she pressed into my lips. My eyes closed as I thought of being so close to Sarah in my hotel room. I could still smell her; feel the heat from her body. Even though she'd pushed me away, I still felt that a part of her had wanted to pull me closer . . . or had I just imagined it?

"I need to get some strange." Chris began scanning the joint for women. "All this lovey-dovey shit is making me horny."

Donna reached out and smacked him on the arm as he laughed at her. I kept a smile on my face, trying to mask the emptiness I felt inside. Maybe everyone was right. What was the harm in letting someone else in and taking my mind off Sarah? At least then she wouldn't view me as a threat to her relationship, and I could still be near her. Maybe then we could just go back to being friends . . . and that would just have to be enough.

I dropped my hand to Donna's thigh and rubbed over her jeans as I listened to the twins talk about new bands. Derek grew louder and more animated as he drank and argued over what the best band of all time was.

I felt my eyes drift to Sarah, who was deep in her own thoughts. Her dark hair was wild and messy around her face. She looked as if she'd just stepped off the beach or . . . I shook the thought of what she had been doing with Derek from my mind. Her eyes met mine as if she sensed I was thinking about her.

Terry's hand clapped down on my shoulder. He had said something and I didn't hear it.

"What?" I called out, trying to crane my neck to see him.

"Let's play some pool."

I nodded as Donna slid off my lap and I stood up behind her, my hands on her small waist. She had no idea how much easier she made all of this on me. Her friendship was the only thing keeping me off a ledge tonight. She glanced over her shoulder at me, smiling as her hand fell on mine, and she laced our fingers together, giving my hand a squeeze.

"You ready to get your ass kicked?" I asked next to her ear so only she could hear.

"As long as I don't end up looking like Derek when you're done with me," she joked sarcastically as we made our way to the tables.

"He got off easy." I sighed as I ran my free hand through my messy hair.

"That's what she said," Chris said quietly as he walked by.

CHAPTER Ten

SARAH

I HAD THE OVERWHELMING urge to write. My fingers burned to put ink to paper to try to sort out everything that was on my mind.

I sat down at a small table along the wall, and Donna took the seat on the other side as we watched the guys prepare for their game of pool.

"You all right?" she asked as I drummed my fingers on the table.

"Just thinking of some lyrics." I smiled politely at her as my eyes went back to the guys. E and Terry were on one team against Derek and Chris. They were already taking jabs at each other as Chris broke.

"I wish I could put words down on a paper and have it come out as a beautiful song."

"Some of the most beautiful songs come from pain," I said sullenly as my eyes danced over E, who was bent over the table and lining up his shot.

"You and E are close, huh?"

Her words caught me off guard, and I quickly looked down at the chipping black paint on my nails. "We're just friends." I regretted using the word *just*, but Donna ignored it.

She nodded and took a sip from her beer as her eyes followed E around the pool table. "I'm worried about him."

"Why? What did he say?" My voice rose an octave.

"You know E." Her eyes fell to mine and she smiled sadly. "He doesn't say much. But when he gets down, it is nearly impossible to pull him out of it. He doesn't open up."

E walked over, pool stick in hand, and grabbed Donna's beer from the table, winking at her as he picked it up and put it to his lips.

"You winning?" she asked,

He smiled with a quick nod. He glanced at me but quickly looked back to Donna and kissed her on the forehead. "I'm doing all right."

She smiled and reached out to run the pad of her thumb over the small cut on Eric's bottom lip. "That looks like it hurts."

"You should see the other guy." He winked as he tucked her hair behind her ear and turned around to watch the game.

I picked at the chipping paint from my pinkie nail and watched the flake flutter to the dirty wooden floor as I hummed to myself.

"I'll be right back," E called to Donna and disappeared into the main bar area.

A few minutes later he returned with a pen and a piece of paper from an order pad. He set them down next to me and his lips curved up slightly.

I stopped humming, realizing that he had heard me.

"Write it down," he said quietly, and turned back to the pool game. My heart stuttered at how well he knew me.

I flipped the paper over in my hand before jotting down a few lines.

I drove all night trying to escape,

the truth of you I cannot take,

on E and broken-down,

why is that bad luck follows when you come around?

"Get me a beer?" My eyes shot up to Derek's and I nodded as I crumbled the paper and tossed it on the table.

I slid off my stool and made my way into the crowded bar. Country music blared from the speakers and I bobbed my head to the beat as I waited for the bartender to notice me. Fingers trailed over my lower back, followed by the unmistakable smell of E's cologne. My body stiffened but his hand fell away, an easy smile on his face.

He leaned in closer to my ear so I could hear him over the noise. "You all right?" His breath against my neck gave me a chill.

"I'm fine." I stared ahead at the cash register.

"Nothing's changed." His voice was lower, and I knew exactly what he was referring to.

"I know. I promise I'm fine." Everything seemed to have changed. He nodded and held up his hand to get the bartender's attention. She made her way over to us, leaning over the wooden top toward E.

"Six buds, please."

Her eyes drifted lower to where his shirt stretched tight over his chest. "Coming right up." She turned to grab the beers from the fridge behind her and E laughed.

"What?" I snapped.

"Why do you look so pissed off?"

"I'm not. I was just thinking." Why the hell was I pissed off? Women looked at E all of the time.

The bartender set the beers in front of us. I tried to grab money from my pocket, but E put his hand on my arm and slowly shook his head no as he pulled his wallet from his back pocket.

"I don't need you to buy my beer." I grabbed three of the bottles as he set money on the bar, and he grabbed the other three.

"I know you don't."

We made our way through the crowd and I managed not to

spill beer all over myself. I gave a bottle to Chris and held one out to Derek. He took it without a glance and drank it half down.

"You could at least say thank you," I snapped.

"Thank you." His voice dripped with sarcasm but he was smiling sweetly.

"Not to me. To E. He bought it for you." I rolled my eyes as I glanced over at the table. E was standing in front of Donna, his head bent down close to her, and I couldn't tell if they were kissing. Derek's gaze followed mine as he ran the chalk over the end of his stick.

"He looks happy."

"Yeah . . . he does."

His face studied mine for a moment. "So why don't *you*?" His eyes were narrowed and his beer-laced breath blew across my face.

"I am." I tried to hide my frustration with him from my voice, but I was sure he caught it. "I'm just exhausted."

This caused him to smile and he pressed his body against my side. "We did have quite a workout earlier." His lips pressed against my neck and I leaned into his touch, closing my eyes as his arm slipped around my waist.

"Want to play another game?" E asked, and I opened my eyes to see him standing behind Donna, his hands on her shoulders. "I think the twins gave up." He motioned with his chin, and I turned around to see Chris and Terry in a deep conversation with the women at the table behind us.

"Couples?" Derek asked with an eyebrow cocked.

"I don't even know how to play." Donna shook her head, and E pressed his mouth against her hair and said something in her ear, but his eyes watched me.

"Just us," E called out. "Unless you're afraid I'll kick your ass," he added with a laugh, and Donna brought her elbow back into his side and shook her head.

Derek laughed humorlessly and shot him a pointed glare. I knew I would never hear the end of his hatred for E when we got back to our room. "Not afraid, man. Not as long as I got my good-luck charm beside me." Derek kissed my neck again, but it wasn't soft and sweet as it had been a moment ago. He was clearly marking his territory, keeping his glare squarely on E.

"Want to make it interesting?" E's fingers moved softly against Donna's shoulders, but tension was obvious in his grip, too.

"Name your terms."

CHAPTER
Eleven

ERIC

IT WAS NO secret that Derek couldn't walk away from a bet, and after last night I still didn't feel satisfied that he had learned his lesson. I wouldn't always be there to stop him from hurting Sarah, but maybe I could make her see that he wasn't as good to her as she thought. It was starting to feel as if she'd never figure it out on her own. Maybe this wasn't the best way to get back into the friend zone with Sarah, but right now it felt more important to get her away from that cheating asshole. Show her what a dick he really was.

"You want to go see what we can find on the jukebox?" Donna called over to Sarah.

She nodded, but turned to Derek. "Keep it friendly." She kissed him on the lips, and his hand slid down over her ass as he deepened the kiss.

I clenched my jaw as I waited for the girls to walk away out of earshot.

"Loser has to get a tattoo. Whatever the winner picks, wherever the winner picks. Just no face ink." Derek was nearly head to toe with tattoos, and I didn't have anything. I knew it was a risky move, but I wanted to prove a point. Hopefully, at the end of the night, neither of us would be getting inked.

Chris came to stand by my side and cocked an eyebrow as he heard the bet.

"Either way I win." Derek laughed and grabbed the balls from the slot underneath the table, and I knew he wasn't just talking about the tat.

"Interesting bet," Chris said as he cracked his knuckles.

I nodded, sipping my beer. "I know what I'm doing."

"Since when?"

"Just shut up and watch." I shook my head and grabbed a stick.

THE BEER FLOWED freely and I was keeping the game pretty evenly paced to this point. The more I drank, the more I relaxed and joked around with everyone. Everything felt as it had months ago while we were on tour. Derek and I had never liked each other, but we tolerated each other. I pretended that nothing bothered me.

That was until Derek's hand slid up Sarah's bare thigh. I began to focus on the game and sank one shot after another.

When I knocked the last ball into the corner pocket, Donna

wrapped her arms around my neck and kissed my cheek. I had to give it to her, she was one hell of an actress. Derek tossed his stick on the table angrily and mumbled something about me cheating. I laughed at the absurdity of his accusing someone else of cheating and sat my beer on the edge of the table.

"I'm just better than you," I called out as he walked away from Sarah, and she glared over at me.

"It's just a stupid game," she said as she grabbed his arm to stop him from storming off, but he pulled from her grip.

"Fuck him," he snapped as he looked over her shoulder to me. "I don't know how you could be friends with that prick."

I waited to hear Sarah defend our friendship, but she didn't say anything.

"Let's go get this over with." He stepped closer to the table.

Sarah looked from Derek to me, confused. "Get what over with?"

He just shook his head.

"You not gonna follow through?" I asked, knowing damn well he wouldn't let me get the best of him. Not after I'd just embarrassed him in front of his girlfriend.

"Let's fucking do it. What do you have in mind?"

I pretended to think it over. "I'll figure it out when we get to the tattoo parlor."

"You bet a tattoo?" Sarah asked, narrowing her eyes at me. I nodded but avoided her glare. I knew exactly what she was thinking. I didn't have any because I refused to put something permanent on my skin when everything in my life to this point had always been so temporary.

"Fuck it. Let's go," Derek mumbled.

I grinned.

"What are you up to?" Donna asked quietly as we made our way toward the exit.

I pressed a kiss into her hair. "You'll see."

She shook her head but didn't press any further. As we walked down the main drag toward Tit for Tat, Chris and Terry had a field day fucking with Derek about what I should make him get. Some of the more humiliating ones were tempting.

As we reached the door to the parlor, I pulled it open, waiting for everyone else to step inside. Sarah glared at me again but didn't say anything.

I walked up to the shop manager and asked if he had any openings. The tattoo would be small and wouldn't take long, so they said they could take us.

"What are you trying to get and where?" the manager asked as he put on his black-frame glasses. He reminded me of Clark Kent, only covered in ink.

I glanced over to Derek and raised an eyebrow. He pulled his shirt over his head and I examined the bare patches of skin.

"Chest will do. Right over the heart. I'll make this easy on you since you did have the balls to come down and do this. Says a lot about what kind of man you are." But I knew what he did next would really tell the truth about who he was. "Get Sarah's name. Any font you like. I'll buy."

The look in his eyes was priceless. For a guy covered in the dumbest fucking tattoos imaginable, it was shocking he would hesitate, but I knew he would. A part of me almost felt guilty. I knew this would hurt Sarah. I knew it was a dick move. But I also knew it would force him to show his true scumbag colors to her.

Sarah's eyes grew wide and her mouth fell open slightly. I looked down at Derek, towering over him by a good six inches and my frame at least twice as wide. He flicked the long hair from his face and his lip twitched. I had him backed into a corner. He would either have to get the tat to avoid upsetting Sarah or he would hit another nail into the coffin of their relationship.

"That's stupid. I already have a tat for her." He pointed to his arm, which had a black star in the same place Sarah had her tattoo that read ROCK.

"What's one more?" I shrugged.

Derek didn't respond, and Sarah turned, shoved open the door to the outside, and disappeared past the shop windows.

"What the fuck is your problem?" Derek took a step forward, getting in my face.

"I'm not the one who just pissed off my girlfriend."

"That's right. *You're* the one who pissed off *my* girlfriend."

As much as I hated to admit it, that stung. I knew Derek wouldn't go through with that kind of commitment to her. I knew it would hurt her when he didn't, but through the alcohol haze, I only saw exposing him for what he was.

Chris's hand clamped on my shoulder, and Terry stepped up behind Derek.

"Pissing match is over. Let's get the fuck out of here." Chris kept his voice low so we wouldn't disrupt other customers.

Derek sneered at me and turned to the door, slamming it open and disappearing into the night.

"What the hell was that?" Terry asked as he shook his head and laughed.

"I had to. Sarah thinks he is some kind of fucking hero after last night. It was this or hit him again." I shrugged as I opened the door and waited for Donna to walk out.

"Do you think he went after her to make sure she makes it back okay?" Everyone stopped and just looked at me as if I had grown another head. "I'll call her. You guys can go ahead."

"I'll text you where we go," Donna said as Terry looped his arm over her shoulder and they began to walk across the street.

I pulled my phone from my pocket along with a crumbled piece of paper I had forgotten about. I held it in my palm as I called her and hoped she would answer.

After two attempts, she finally did and she wasn't happy. "What?" she snapped.

I took a deep breath. "Where are you?"

"Oh, I don't know, E. I'm at the corner of Pissed Off and Go Fuck Yourself."

"Fair enough. I know I deserved that."

"You humiliated me. Why would you do that? Huh? What if you would have lost? Would you have gotten a tattoo?"

I shut my eyes as I silently berated myself for being so fucking stupid. Having Sarah angry at me sobered me up quickly. "The real question is, why didn't Derek?"

The line went silent and I pulled it back from my ear to make sure she hadn't hung up.

"I'm fucking sorry. I shouldn't have done that. I never meant to hurt you."

"That is exactly what you meant to do."

The line went dead and I struggled not to throw my cell phone and bust it into a million pieces. I clenched my fist, crumbling the scrap of paper tighter. I slipped my phone into my pocket and un-folded the paper as my eyes danced over the familiar handwriting.

I drove all night trying to escape,
the truth of you I cannot take,
on E and broken-down,
why is that bad luck follows when you come around?

My mind raced as I read it half a dozen times. Was she talking about me? It clearly said *on E*, but that could have meant exactly what it said. There it was, the dull ache in the back of my mind. But then I reread the line about bad luck and I couldn't help but feel I had destroyed our friendship.

I took off down the street, needing desperately to forget everyone and everything. As I neared the end of the block and turned the corner toward the hotel, I stopped at the sight of Sarah, her head in her hands as she cried quietly to herself.

"Sarah . . ." I wrapped my arms around her and she pulled away from me, but I tightened my grip, holding her against my chest.

"Get off me," she sobbed as her tears continued to flow.

"I'm not letting go."

"You should. Derek is the one that should be hugging me right now."

The mention of his name infuriated me. For the millionth time, I considered telling her what Derek had done last night. But I knew that would only make things worse. Unless she saw it for herself, she'd never believe me. Especially not now.

And it's not as if I had any solid proof to show her—it was my word, my obviously jealous word, against his.

"But he's not here, Sarah, I am." I rubbed my hand down her back trying to calm her. "Friends hug. Let me hold you."

"It's not the same." She looked up at me through sad, tear-filled eyes. I brushed her hair back from her damp face.

"I know you would rather it was him here. I'm sorry."

"No. I mean *this* isn't the same." Her eyes burned with rage as she gestured between us. I was suddenly aware of her breasts pressed against me, the fruity smell of her shampoo. We were completely alone in the alley and she wasn't struggling to get away from me anymore. Instead, she was studying my eyes, a look of pain on her face. "We were great friends. Why would you mess that up?"

"Hey, it was *you* who spent weeks dodging *my* calls and clearly trying to cut *me* out. I wasn't the one that ruined it."

Wrong thing to say.

"Are you fucking kidding me? So that's what all of this is? You're trying to get back at me for not calling you? You're such a *girl* sometimes."

I laughed and it only pissed her off more, but I couldn't help it. Did she really have no idea how I felt about her?

"You think I kissed you to get back at you? You think the bet was to get back at you?"

"You tell me."

I wanted to tell her everything, lay it all on the line, but she might never talk to me again. Instead, I tried to make things go back to before the tour ended. Having her in my life and watching her with someone else was still better than not having her around at all.

"I didn't mean to fuck up our friendship, Sarah." I shook my head, hating that I was hurting her. "Forget everything I said. I promise you I will leave you alone while you're here."

I reluctantly took a step back from her and let my arms fall from her body.

She didn't say a word as she turned and walked away toward the end of the block. I watched as she slipped farther away and turned the corner. I balled my hand into a fist and swung at the wall where she had just stood in my arms. Pain shot up to my elbow as my knuckles cracked against the brick.

CHAPTER
Twelve

SARAH

I NEEDED TO GET as far away from E as possible so he wouldn't know that my tears were because of him. Why did he have to kiss me? He was one of my best friends, and now I couldn't be around him without thinking about his lips against mine. I hated myself for even having the thought and for forcing me to lie to Derek.

Making it to my room, I collapsed on the bed, curling up into a ball and sobbing. The sheets still smelled like Derek and my stomach turned. I knew I couldn't be here when he came back. I needed to escape, run away from everyone. I had done it once before and I could do it again.

I tried to ignore the way E had made me feel; tried to ignore the stabbing pain in my gut when he held Donna in his arms, looking at her the way I wished he would look at me. He was clearly happy with her. Why couldn't he just let me be happy with Derek? Was he really that pissed off about my not calling him? I wanted to tell him that it was Derek who didn't want me to talk to him, but that would only make him and Derek hate each other more. I was only here for two weeks, but when I left, it would just be Derek and me and I couldn't lose him.

"Why couldn't you just get the fucking tattoo?" I mumbled to myself as I stared down through blurry eyes at the tattoo on my arm. I ran my fingers over the raised lines that I had put there, what felt like a lifetime ago.

Each one like an eraser for the pain that had coursed through my body. I slid the pad of my index finger over each one as I closed my eyes and remembered the situations that had caused me to cut myself. They all paled in comparison to how I felt right now.

I pushed to my feet, stumbled as I made my way to the hotel minibar. I grabbed the first little bottle I saw. Jack Daniel's. I poured it back against my throat, begging for it to take the edge off. I didn't want to hurt like this and I didn't want to do the one thing I knew would relieve the pain.

I grabbed another bottle and drank that one, too, coughing as the taste made me gag and nearly vomit. I froze when I heard voices in the hallway, hoping it wasn't Derek. They continued on; their muffled laughter faded away. I grabbed another drink, struggling with the cap before I finished off that one, too.

"Please work . . . please work . . ." I pushed to my feet and made my way to the bathroom, ramming my shoulder into the doorframe as I tripped over the towel I had left on the floor earlier when I was with Derek. "Aah . . . ," I cried out, knowing it would bruise.

I stepped inside the bathroom and slammed the door angrily and caught sight of my reflection in the mirror. My heavy eyeliner had smeared down my cheeks. I was breathing heavily, unable to calm myself down. I gripped the sides of the sink, using it to keep myself from collapsing on the floor in tears.

My body was begging for me to release the sadness in the one way that I knew would work. I squeezed my eyes shut hard as I struggled against my secret demons. "I'm as free as a bird now . . ."

I was singing loudly along with Lynyrd Skynyrd as they belted out "Free Bird." I didn't even hear him enter and creep up behind me.

"You're growing up into a pretty little thing." Phil smiled sickeningly, his teeth showing like a rabid dog's. I crossed my arms over my chest, hating that at twelve my body had begun to change and so had the way Phil acted toward me.

"Please leave me alone, Phil."

He reached out, tucking my hair behind my ear, his fingers trailing down my cheek. I wanted to pull away from his touch, but I was frozen in fear. His tongue ran out over his lower lip and I shivered, my stomach rolling as I opened my mouth to scream for my mom, but no sound came out.

"Sarah!" My little sister came barreling into my bedroom, coming to a stop as she saw Phil standing in front of me, his hand still on my face. He turned to look over Jenny and his smile grew.

"What is it, Jenny?" My voice shook, and my eyes locked on Phil.

"Come play with me!"

It was killing me that I couldn't call the one person I knew would understand, E. I kept the real me carefully concealed from most of the world, but he could always see the sadness that lurked under the surface, reflecting back his own. He was also the only one in the world who knew how bad things were for me growing up.

My phone rang and I listened to it as I stared at my reflection in the mirror. I hated the person who stared back at me. She was weak and a liar. She wasn't strong and independent the way she claimed to be onstage.

The phone silenced and I shook my head as a fresh wave of sobs racked my body. I sank to the floor and grabbed the towel from it and ran the corner of it under the cold water. I began to scrub the black smudges from my face, wishing I could do the same to my soul.

When all of the makeup that I hid behind was gone, it was like looking at a completely different person. I was the girl in my school pictures, hair slightly longer, with the same broke smile and sad eyes, hiding a sickening secret from the world. I gathered my hair at the back of my head and pulled it up into a loose ponytail.

I would never look as sophisticated as Donna, but maybe it was time I changed who I was. I wasn't enough for E and for damn sure was not enough to keep Derek from running off. I looked down at my stupid schoolgirl skirt and tank top accented with safety pins to give it a punk edge. I stripped off my shirt and slid my skirt down my legs. I ran my finger over the top of my thigh, tracing the thin, pink line that was fresher than the other scars, but was healing nicely. No one had asked about that one because the only person who ever saw that part of me ignored it. He pretended it didn't exist.

I looked at myself, naked with only a pair of black, boy-cut underwear. I ran my hand over my stomach. Hating how it stuck out, hating that my hips were narrower than I liked.

The alcohol was beginning to take the edge off the pain, but it wasn't enough. I made my way back to the minibar and collapsed to my knees as I grabbed another bottle and drank it down without flinching. I drank several more until my head swam and my skin began to tingle.

Derek had carried my cigarettes so I dug through his bag to find another pack. When I couldn't locate them, I stood up with it and turned it upside down. Scattering the contents all over the floor and on top of the minibottles of memory loss.

I grabbed a pack and tore it open, throwing the trash on the floor as I made my way to the tiny kitchen area. I turned on one of the burners to the stove and waited for it to heat up. As it glowed bright orange, I stuck the cigarette between my lips and leaned down, pressing the tip to the hot surface. I wobbled on my feet and stuck my hand out to catch myself, placing the tip of my finger right on the glowing spot.

I yanked back my finger, at first wondering why it felt ice-cold. Within a second I realized that I had burned myself and my fingertip was throbbing in agony. Fresh tears sprang to my eyes as I waved it around frantically, trying to get rid of the hurt.

CHAPTER

Thirteen

ERIC

THERE IS NOT enough whiskey in the world to drown out the feeling of having your heart ripped out of your fucking chest. I knew that Sarah couldn't be left alone in her sadness and anger or she would self-destruct. I grabbed my phone from my pocket and stared at the screen. I wondered if he was with her now or if she was all alone. I struggled against my instinct to protect her. She'd made it clear that she didn't want me to be that person. I flexed my fingers, the skin of my bruised knuckles pulling apart and sending a sharp jab of pain up my arm.

"Leave her be. She will call you if she needs you." Donna took the phone from my hands and slid it into the back of her jeans.

"She's not going to call me, Donna." I sighed heavily as I drank back the shot in front of me.

She grabbed my good hand and pulled me from the barstool toward the door. "Let's get some fresh air."

As we stepped out onto the sidewalk, I pulled a cigarette from my pack and lit it. I blew out a heavy cloud of smoke as I watched the cars pass by.

Donna leaned against the wall, her eyes bloodshot and unfocused from trying to match me shot for shot. I watched her as she looked up at a hotel across the street, half the windows still lit from the lights inside. I put my arm around her shoulders and pulled her to my side.

"Thank you," I whispered in her hair.

"For what?" She looked up at me, her face dangerously close to mine.

"For being here." I dropped my cigarette to the ground and brought my hand up to push the hair back from her face. Her eyes closed and reopened slowly as I touched her skin. I leaned closer as I studied her expression. She didn't try to pull away from me as her tongue rolled over her lips, wetting them and causing them to glisten from the dim neon light that hung overhead. Her reaction to me was the polar opposite of Sarah's. She wasn't repulsed or hurt by my touch, and I needed more than anything to feel wanted. By anyone.

I pushed my mouth against hers, needing to feel the tenderness, the acceptance of someone else. Her eyes fell closed again and her lips parted as I ran my tongue over them. My hand slid into her long hair, my fingers twisting in its softness as I held her to my mouth. She moaned softly, her hand falling on my chest. I pulled her against me as I deepened our kiss, her own tongue exploring mine.

There was a need, a longing, in the way she moved against me, and I wanted so desperately to give her the escape we both sought.

I reluctantly pulled away from our kiss to look into her eyes, the unasked question answered as her mouth found mine again. This time her kiss was more eager and I couldn't help but push her back against the wall as I pressed my hips into her, letting her feel how much I needed her.

I ran my hands down her body, brushing against her breasts and down her narrow waist. I slid one hand behind her, grabbing her ass as the other lifted her thigh and gave me better access to her. I groaned as I rocked my hips into her, the jeans causing an unbearable friction between us. She gasped into my mouth and it only made me get more lost in her.

"Can I take you to my room?" My breathing was erratic and I had to force myself from finishing right here what we'd started.

She nodded, her cheeks flushed and lips swollen from our kisses. I pulled my body back from hers, hating the emptiness without her against me. I wrapped her fingers in mine as I guided us down the sidewalk and back to the hotel.

We crossed the lobby quickly, and when we got into the elevator, I smiled as I leaned against the wall and pulled her between my legs so I could kiss her again. Her fingers slid under the edge of my shirt and ran along the top of my jeans as our kisses became needier. The doors opened and we didn't break apart as someone stepped into the elevator with us and cleared his throat. We both smiled and pressed against each other as we rose another floor, and the doors opened again. I backed her out of the tiny space and we stumbled and laughed. It felt so good to let go, to let myself get close to someone, have fun with someone . . .

"Sorry," I called out behind me to the stranger as Donna giggled and tugged at the buckle of my jeans. I kept my arm looped around her back so she wouldn't fall as we continued down the hall and fell against my door.

I grabbed the key card from my pocket and tried unsuccessfully to stick it in the slot in the door. Donna took it from my hand and spun around to give it a try. I gripped her hips, pulling her ass back against me. She laughed and pulled on the handle, shoving the door open. We nearly fell inside but I held on to her, lifting her in my arms and kicking the door closed behind me.

I walked her straight to the bed and sat her down in the center. The air around us changed in this private space with only the two of us. As I stood in front of her as she sat on the edge of the bed, I wondered if we would regret this in the morning. Sensing my hesitation, Donna grabbed my jeans and pulled me closer. She slowly undid the button as she gazed up at me, lust in her eyes.

I fought back the thought that I was going to lose her, too, if I went through with this. But as she pulled down my zipper and reached inside my boxers, all rational thought escaped me.

MY HEAD WAS pounding and I rubbed my forehead trying to force my eyes open. A leg slid over my waist and I froze as I glanced beside me to the mess of dark hair. My fingers gripped her knee and I leaned over, slowly brushing her hair from her face. Donna was sleeping peacefully beside me, and flashes of the night before slowly crept back into my memory. I slowly slid out from under her leg and got out of bed, suddenly aware of how naked I was.

I grabbed my boxers from the floor and slid them on as I made my way into the bathroom. I splashed cold water on my face, unable to look at myself in the mirror. The consequences of our night together were going to be too much for me to handle. I couldn't lose another friend.

I leaned over the sink as I let the water droplets fall from my face, my hands clinging to the porcelain until the cuts on my knuckles pulled open.

A hand slid around my waist and I closed my eyes as I took in the severity of what I'd done. I was beyond wasted and I knew Donna was, too. I had had no right to take advantage of her.

"I'm so sorry," I whispered, my voice rough from the night of partying. Her hand froze on my stomach.

"Why are you sorry?" She sounded so small and fragile and I wanted to wrap my arms around her.

"I shouldn't have taken advantage of you." I shook head, mentally chastising myself.

"You had just as much to drink as I had."

"That doesn't matter." I turned around to face Donna and froze as I gazed down at her naked body. I hated myself for the way my body immediately reacted.

There was a knock at the door and we both looked over at it

before her eyes fell back on mine. I put my finger to her lips to tell her to be quiet.

She didn't say a word, and I slipped out of the bathroom and closed the door behind me. I took a deep breath before pulling open the door to the hallway.

Derek stood on the other side and my body tensed as I resisted the urge to punch him in the fucking mouth.

"Can we talk?"

I sighed loudly as I took a step back to let him enter, my eyes briefly flicking to the bathroom door as I walked over to the bed and sat on the edge. Derek stood in front of me as he gazed around the room. I gestured to the chair at a small desk and he nodded, pulling it out and taking a seat. I found my jeans by my feet and grabbed my cigarettes and lit one as I groaned.

"This shit between us needs to stop."

I cocked an eyebrow at his tone as I took a drag, but didn't respond.

"I know what you think of me and the feeling is mutual, but Sarah doesn't need this shit. She was a fucking mess when I came home this morning."

He had spent the night out without her. I couldn't resist the urge to make a dig at him. "Classy." I stretched my back, feeling as if I had been hit by a train.

His eyes danced around the room at the piles of clothes that obviously weren't all mine.

"That goes both ways." He pushed to his feet. "I'm telling you to stay the fuck away from both of us. And if you do have to come around, keep it civil. You're only hurting her."

I pushed to my feet as I ran my hand through my hair. I was not about to be threatened by this asshole who caused Sarah more pain then anyone else I knew. But her words from last night came back to me and I knew she wanted me to stay away as well. It wasn't just him.

"You done?"

He glanced down at his feet as he shoved his hands in his pockets. I followed his gaze to Donna's tank top, the same one from last night that read DAMAGED across the chest. Recognition flashed in his eyes and he glanced to the bathroom door.

"Yeah." He smiled. "We're done." With that he turned and left, slamming the door behind him.

I sighed as I sat back on the bed and took another drag of my cigarette.

Donna came out of the bathroom, a white towel wrapped around her body. "I should go to my room and shower, get clean clothes."

I looked up at her and nodded, unable to find the words to tell her what we had done should never have happened; would never happen again.

I watched as she gathered her clothes and slipped back into the bathroom to put them on, before disappearing out into the hallway.

I made my way into the bathroom and found my phone sitting on the counter. I slid my finger over the screen and saw six unread messages from Sarah. My heart stopped as I opened them to read.

CHAPTER

Fourteen

SARAH

I'D SPENT THE last hour in bed feeling as if I had been
kicked in the head by a horse. I have no idea what
time Derek had come back to the room, but he was by my side
when I woke. I blinked my eyes open and saw his staring back at
me, concern on his face.

"What?" I asked, trying not to sound upset.

"What happened?"

"Nothing." I shrugged as I looped my hand in his.

"You trashed the room, killed the minibar, and the stove
was on."

I closed my eyes, knowing that no excuses could make me
sound sane in this situation. Part of me wanted to ask him why

he cared. Why now? But I bit my tongue because I craved this side of him more than anything else.

"I was upset."

"Then we will make it better." He pulled my hand to his lips and kissed the back of it gently. "Take a shower. It will help."

I gave him a small smile as I slipped out of bed and into the bathroom. As soon as my eyes locked on my phone, I could feel the panic spread from my chest. I picked it up and scrolled through the messages I had sent to E last night before I passed out.

> I need you right now.
> I can't do this anymore.
> Please . . . I'm not a free . . .

I shut the phone, unable to read the rest. Derek must have seen them. His clothes from last night were on the floor. I turned on the water to the shower, holding my breath as a few tears slid down my cheeks. After a minute I heard the door to the hotel hallway open and close quietly. I knew he was going to talk to E, and any hope I had of saving my friendship was gone.

I slid off my underwear and stepped into the scalding-hot water. I had fucked up things beyond repair last night. There was no going back with E, and now Derek was going to make sure of it. I dipped my head into the stream of water and held my breath as it washed over my face.

I grabbed a washrag and lathered it with soap before scrubbing hard over my skin. I wanted to erase the night, erase the scars, erase my past.

I stood under the spray until my skin pruned and my body shivered uncontrollably as I got out and wrapped a towel around myself.

Derek was sitting on the bed, his elbows on his knees and his head hanging as I stepped out. He looked up at me, and instead of being angry, he smiled. "I didn't think you were ever getting out." The unusual cheerfulness to his tone made me uncomfortable, as if he were deliberately ignoring my pain, or laughing in the face of it. "Get dressed. We have dinner with Tucker and Cass today. I know you don't want to miss that."

I couldn't help but make a face. E would be at a dinner with Tucker. I stepped farther into the bedroom space and sank down to dig around my bag for something to wear. I decided on a pair of jeans and a formfitting T-shirt. I glanced back at Derek over my shoulder; he was watching me intently.

I stood with my back to him as I dropped my towel and pulled on a pair of underwear.

Derek laughed to himself as I continued to get dressed, and I was scared to even ask him what was on his mind. He didn't leave me to guess.

"If you had messaged me, I would have been here, babe."

I froze with my pants midway up my thighs.

"Really. No need to bug E while he's getting it on with Donna."

I pulled my pants up slowly, glad I was not facing him so he could get the satisfaction of my reaction.

"I didn't realize he was." I hated that my voice wavered.

"They are dating. Don't worry. He wasn't that pissed. I smoothed it over."

I pulled my shirt over my head and turned to face Derek as I grabbed my wet hair and freed it from the collar of my shirt. I gave him my best fake smile that I showed everyone else. "Thank you. I can be stupid when I drink."

"It's fine, babe. He understood."

I cringed inwardly at the thought of Derek's talking to E about me. And the thought of him with Donna while I was texting him last night . . . suddenly I felt nauseous again.

"Where's the dinner?" I examined the burn on my fingertip, which was now pink and swollen, but hadn't blistered.

"Have to ask the twins. I haven't heard from him. I just know afterwards we're gonna hit the strip club to make up for him not having a bachelor party."

I dug through my bag and grabbed my hairbrush, running it through my hair absentmindedly as I thought about how badly I had broken down last night. I hadn't had that happen for a long time, and I felt that I was starting to slip back into the person I used to be. At least today I could pull Cass aside and have someone to talk to. I needed to vent, to sort out what I was feeling.

If I had not passed out last night, I would have hurt myself. It wasn't a matter of if but when.

"We can skip the dinner if you want."

I sighed as my heart sank. "No. It's fine," I lied, dropping my brush in my bag.

His arms wrapped around my waist from behind and his lips pressed against my neck. "Is it?"

I could only nod.

He spun me around to face him, his eyes searching mine for the truth. He sighed, his shoulders sagging. "We can just leave. My brother's been bugging me to come see him in Texas."

"I want to stay. I want to see Cass."

He nodded, pushing the wet hair from my face. "Maybe afterward. I think it would be good for us to get away from all of this."

"Yeah . . . maybe."

He pulled me against his chest and I wrapped my arms around his neck. Spending some time alone with Derek and away from the partying was exactly what we needed. When things aren't this hectic, we actually enjoy each other's company. I missed that. Missed us.

"I'm gonna run through the shower and get ready."

I reluctantly let go of him as he disappeared into the bathroom. I sank down on the bed and dropped my head in my hands. How had everything gotten so fucked-up in such a short time?

I needed to get it out before it consumed me. I found my old, tattered notebook and sat down at the small desk at the foot of the bed.

The flames lick at my fingertips as I'm drawn to the fire,

I want to run but I'm consumed by the overwhelming desire,

To let you in and break apart these walls,

That contain me, don't blame me, I'm trying not to fall,

But it hurts to ignore it and it hurts to lie,

By myself in this bed when I'm starting to cry.

My mind was racing as I tried to get everything out that I had been keeping in so long. It was like therapy to me, and as I confessed my pain, I was confessing something else as well, but I was too scared to admit it.

"You're writing."

I turned around to see Derek running his hand through his long, dark hair, a towel slung low on his hips. My eyes danced over his tattoos and the bare spot on his chest. It was a perfect representation of how empty his heart was.

"Just jotting down some lyrics. We could use some new material for the next tour."

He nodded as he gathered some clothes from the floor.

"I'm sorry." I was apologizing for the mess I had made. The mess of my life.

"Me, too." He tossed his towel on the bed and I turned around to stare at the paper in front of me.

CHAPTER

Fifteen

ERIC

RUBBED MY HAND along my jaw as I stared at the messages from Sarah. How could I have left her alone last night? What did she mean she wasn't free?

R u ok?

I hit send and made my way into the small kitchen area to get myself a glass of water. Visions of last night danced through the edge of my memory. In forty-eight hours, I had effectively destroyed things with Sarah from all sides. The kiss, the dare, the night with Donna . . . Sarah had reached out to me and I hadn't even known because I was busy fucking up my friendship with Donna, too. By the time this trip was over, I would have no one left. My phone vibrated in my palm and my heart raced as I slid my finger over the screen.

I'm fine. Sorry I bothered u.

I stared at the words as if they would change before my eyes. I typed out a quick response: You don't bother me.

I set my glass in the sink and ran my hand over the back of my neck, rubbing away the tightness in my muscles. The phone vibrated again.

I shouldn't have texted u. I won't ever again.

"Fuck," I threw my phone, and the back flew off as it hit the wall on the other side of the bed. I needed to get the fuck out of this place before I lost my mind. For months I'd missed her, and now that she was back in my life, I'd pushed her even further away. To make things worse, I would have to face her for the next week and a half while we were all still in LA.

They say what doesn't kill you makes you stronger, but I had never felt as weak as I did now. I wasn't thinking clearly and I needed to take a step back and reevaluate what I was doing.

I decided I needed to get some of my frustration out in the gym. I hadn't worked out in days. I changed into some shorts and a white T-shirt and set off for the gym on the first floor. It was practically empty and I was glad the twins were probably still asleep. I needed to lift, to feel the burn and ache in my muscles, but my head was going crazy.

I jumped on the treadmill and slowly upped the speed until I was full on running, staring at the television mounted in the corner of the room as I let the noise override my thoughts.

The more known our band became, the lonelier life felt. I craved having one person who knew the real me and not the guy on the stage. At least with Tucker off with his new bride, we were able to go out in public without being bothered. But all that would change again today when they finally came back.

As I turned up the speed, the sweat began to run off me, my hair clinging to my forehead as I started to breathe harder.

Trying to run from all of my problems was just like running on this treadmill. You never got anywhere.

I thought of how my family used to be, before my brother was killed. I wanted a family like that for myself, but I knew I was never meant to have that kind of happiness. I wasn't even welcome in my own family. My legs were burning and I forced myself to keep going. I wanted exhaustion. I wanted to wear down my body and hopefully, in the process, my mind.

TWO HOURS LATER I left the gym, my body feeling as if it were ripping in two. I made my way back up to my room, glancing at Donna's door, but deciding now probably wasn't the time to talk about what had happened last night.

I hoped she didn't hate me for what had happened. I didn't think I could handle losing her on top of everything else. I slipped inside my room and took an ice-cold shower, letting the water cool me down until my breathing returned to normal.

I got dressed and grabbed my phone from the floor. It took a minute to locate the back, but I slipped it on and tried to power on. The phone wouldn't work, and the anger that had consumed me earlier returned.

Someone knocked at the door and I groaned as I made my way over to it and yanked it open.

"Dude, what the fuck?" Terry held his hands out to his sides.

"What?"

"You won't answer your phone, you wouldn't answer the door. Donna is freaking out, man. You can't just fuck a chick and ignore her."

"I wasn't ignoring her."

"So you did fuck her? I got to hand it to you, man. Only you could tame the fucking ice queen." He laughed as he slid by me into the room.

I slammed the door and ran my hands through my hair. "I broke my fucking phone and I was in the gym and the shit with Donna is not what you think."

"Yeah, well, we are meeting Tuck down at the Lagoon. Chris already left with Donna."

"Sarah and Derek leave yet?"

"You know, your life is more fucking twisted than a soap opera." Terry pulled open the door and made a sweeping gesture with his hand.

I stepped out into the hall as I laughed. "How the fuck would you know about soap operas?"

"I need my stories, man."

I couldn't help but laugh.

We headed down to the lobby for a waiting cab to take us to the restaurant. I stared out the window the entire drive, not wanting to talk anymore about the female drama. Terry didn't press the issue, but I could tell he was a little more excited than he should be to watch everything unfold. When you spend your life on the road, you have to get your entertainment any way you can.

When we stepped into the lobby, Donna turned to face me. I could see the worry in her eyes. I knew she wasn't sure what my feelings toward her were after last night. I wasn't sure either. I scanned her body, taking in her curves in her simple, formfitting, black dress. I walked over to her and put my arm around her shoulders.

"You look beautiful," I whispered, and her lips quirked into a smile as her hand fell to my chest.

"I wasn't sure you were coming."

"Why would you think that?"

"I thought you'd still be sleeping off your hangover." She shrugged, and our attention turned to the door as Tucker and Cass stepped inside. It felt as if it had been years since we had all been together. We all hugged and congratulated them, making inappropriate comments about their time alone.

"Let's eat. I'm starving." Tucker walked to the hostess and gave her his name. She quickly guided us back into the dining room.

"What did we miss?" he asked as we made our way to the table.

"You don't want to know." I shook my head.

"That bad, huh?"

I waited for Donna to sit before taking the seat next to her. Terry sat on the other side of me. Chris, Tucker, and Cass sat on the other side, leaving two empty seats in front of me, but I wasn't sure Sarah and Derek would even show. She had made it pretty clear she wanted nothing more to do with me.

We ordered drinks as we shared stories about the bar fight and late-night partying. Tuck laughed as we told him about Derek's spending the night in jail, but that was cut short when they finally showed.

Sarah avoided eye contact with me and Derek was being overly friendly.

"Nice of you to show up," Terry joked.

Sarah shook her head. "I couldn't remember the name of the place. I tried to text you." Her gaze met mine for a second and I cocked my head, wondering why she would text me after telling me to leave her alone.

"My phone broke." I picked up my glass of water and took a sip.

"No worries. We're here now." She leaned forward to look over at Cass and smile.

CHAPTER
Sixteen

SARAH

"HOW DOES IT feel being Mrs. Tucker White?" I asked as I held my hair back so it wouldn't drag on my plate.

"It feels . . . like the way it should be." Cass smiled and I loved how genuinely happy she was.

"I still think you should have kept your last name," Chris chimed in as he took a bite from a roll.

"As brilliant of an idea that it was to name our son Jack Daniels, I couldn't go through with it."

Chris put his hand over his heart as if he were hurt, and Cass mouthed sorry to him as she smiled. "I missed this," she said with a sigh as the waitress came over to take our orders. I hadn't even looked over the menu. I picked it up and my eyes scanned the lists of entrées, sneaking a glance at E, who was leaning closer to Donna, discussing what they wanted to eat. Derek's hand fell on my thigh and I looked over at him, smiling weakly as he patted my leg.

He was trying and I hated myself for wishing that he hadn't waited so long to make an effort. I slipped my hand under the table and wrapped my fingers around his and gave them a squeeze.

"I'll have the bacon burger with mayo," I said as I held out my menu for the server to take. She went around the rest of the table taking everyone's order.

After we were left alone again the drinks began to flow, and everyone was in good spirits. For once, there was no fighting, and it made me miss our tour even more.

"Next tour kicks off in a month," Derek said to Tucker.

"We need to have Donna go over our schedule with you. Maybe we can meet up along the way, play a gig together for old times' sake."

"I would love to get to hang out with Cass again. I miss her." I could feel E's eyes on me and I avoided his gaze.

"So you can use me as your Barbie doll again?" Cass laughed and threw a roll toward me.

"Come on. You looked hot and it is always fun to be pampered."

"You did look hot." Tucker gave Cass a lopsided grin and kissed her temple.

"See. It was fun. Plus we could work on some new songs. Have you written anything lately?"

"I wrote a song for Tucker, but I am *not* sharing that with these perverts."

"Can't blame you there. Derek thinks everything has some sort of sexual reference." I rolled my eyes and he elbowed me playfully in the ribs. "It's true."

"It's not my fault you have a dirty mind." He narrowed his eyes and I did the same.

"It would really be nice to have another girl around. Donna is always nose deep in business when we're on the bus."

"Ninety percent of my *business* consists of keeping E out of fights. It's a full-time job," Donna chimed in, and I glanced over toward her, allowing myself to look at E. His eyes were already on mine.

"That's the easy part. You just sidetrack him with a funny story. Once you get him laughing, he forgets all about kicking ass," I replied, and E gave me a lopsided grin.

"I'll keep that in mind. Certainly easier than trying to shove myself between two drunken men while in heels." Donna took a sip from her glass.

The food arrived in the middle of our conversation and everyone quieted down as we ate, except for Terry and Chris, who were arguing over who called dibs on the waitress. They never seemed to tire, and it was exhausting just watching them.

"You could always take turns. It worked out so well for you in the past," E joked, and Terry tossed a roll at him. E picked up a handful of fries and Donna grabbed him, stopping him from starting a food fight in the middle of the restaurant.

"I call first," Chris yelled, and everyone erupted in laughter.

CHAPTER
Seventeen

ERIC

SLIPPED OUTSIDE TO smoke and stared at the pond behind the restaurant. The door opened and I tried not to smile as Sarah stepped out beside me, even though it was physically painful to be near her. Her eyes focused ahead as she leaned against the wall next to me and lit her cigarette.

I flicked my ashes and blew out a puff of smoke. "Look, I'm not going to bother you anymore. But I don't want shit to be weird between us." I cleared my throat. "We were . . . we *are* friends."

"I don't think things have ever *not* been weird." She laughed quietly.

I nodded. "I know you said you didn't want to talk, but I want you to know I'm here if you change your mind."

"When did I say I didn't want to talk?" Her eyes met mine as confusion washed over her face.

The truth dawned on me and I pushed off the wall ready to beat the hell out of Derek. He was playing dirty to keep her and me away from each other. Sarah's hand grabbed my arm to stop me as she studied my face. At least he knew I didn't come and keep her company while he was out all night.

"What are you talking about, E? You're the one who said you would stay away from *me*."

The fight in the alley flashed in my mind, the hurt look in her eyes, and her body against mine as I tried to hold her.

"I shouldn't have said that to you. I'm sorry I wasn't there for you last night. I fucked up." I closed my eyes as I tried to block out the memory of sleeping with Donna. "Tell me what you meant when you said that you aren't free."

"It's fine." Her hand touched my cheek and electricity shot through me. "I'm fine."

My eyes slowly opened as she pulled her hand back from my face. "What happened?" I grabbed her wrists, inspecting the purple, swollen tip of her finger.

"I got in a fight with the stove." She shrugged, looking embarrassed. "You?" She eyed my busted knuckles.

"Brick wall."

She smiled and my finger began to rub over her wrist absentmindedly as I was filled with relief that Sarah wasn't kicking me out of her life. My face slowly inched closer to hers as our breathing picked up. I pulled her finger to my lips and placed a soft kiss on the tip of it. Pink washed over her cheeks as she pulled her lower lip in and ran her teeth over it slowly, and her fingers that still held my arm tightened. There was no staying away from Sarah, and fighting the connection we had was becoming too hard. I knew she felt it. I could see it in the pink of her cheeks, and the smile that played on her lips. She let down her guard, not afraid to let me see the sadness that lingered below the surface, and I did the same. It was freeing. I knew I couldn't turn away even if I wanted to.

"We should go inside before someone comes looking for us," I said quietly, hating that I had to let go of her.

She nodded and we both let our hands fall to our sides as we made our way back in the door. My fingers found the small of her back as she stepped in front of me to enter, but I only let them linger for a second.

Sarah went back to the table but I took a detour to the bathroom, needing to clear my thoughts before having to look at Derek again and to not give him reason to question if we had been together. I would let him believe he had succeeded in making us turn against each other. It was better for Sarah if she didn't have to deal with his jealousy.

I splashed cold water on my face and made my way back to the table. Everyone was talking loudly about the award show performance. Donna smiled over at me, her shoulder bumping into mine. I smiled back, hating that we would eventually have to talk about last night. I dreaded ruining things between us.

I dared a glance across the table. Derek had his arm over Sarah's shoulders as he told Tuck about a show they had done a few weeks ago when the building lost power. Her eyes caught mine and I fought against a smile as I looked down the table at the twins, who were racing to see who could finish his beer the fastest.

I laughed along with the jokes and offered a comment when expected, but all I could think about was Sarah. She wasn't wearing any makeup and her clothes were more everyday than her usual grunge persona. She looked out of place next to Derek, who had on thick liner and whose hair was so black it looked as if it had a blue hue.

"What?" Donna leaned into my side as her eyes studied mine. I shrugged and grabbed my beer, taking a sip. My eyes slid over her perfect porcelain face. She wore makeup, but only to enhance her features, not to hide behind. She took the time to curl her hair and dress to impress. Any man would look at her and think she was beautiful, but my heart didn't stutter when she said my name the way it did with Sarah. I wished it did, it would make things so much simpler. I cared for her a lot and I knew I could be with her and be happy, but it would never be fair to her because I couldn't give her my heart.

"Why don't you like weddings?" I asked, trying to fill the void in conversation between us.

"I . . . uh . . ." Her eyes fell to her lap.

I tipped her chin up with my finger. "I'm sorry. I shouldn't have asked that here." I shook my head. "I wasn't thinking."

"Maybe later?"

"Sure." I smiled, hoping she would open up to me. I knew what it was like not to have someone to share your secrets with.

AFTER WE SETTLED the check, we took several cabs back to the hotel because there we so many of us. I tried to hide my disappointment when I wasn't in the same one as Sarah, but that would have put me in a small space with Derek, and that would have been a bad thing.

We all took off to our rooms to get ready for the night out for the bachelor party. The girls were going to go out for drinks on their own, and Donna was already dressed up so she followed me to my room so we could finish our conversation from earlier.

Everything was as if last night hadn't happened until we stepped inside my room. The bed was still unmade. I cleared my throat and went to dig through my bags. "So . . . weddings," I said as I pulled out a dark gray button-down shirt.

Donna sat on the edge of the bed, her hand running over her leg nervously. "I've just never been a fan."

I pulled my T-shirt over my head as I stretched my sides, still sore from working out. Her eyes slid down my body and back up.

"I was engaged once. This guy named James. We started dating freshman year of college." She paused and I stopped buttoning up my new shirt to look at her, so she knew I was paying attention. "We were together three years. We talked about kids and moving to the suburbs. The American dream." She smiled sadly.

I sat down next to her, nudging her leg with mine. "So what happened?"

"It wasn't a dream, it was a nightmare. The night before our wedding I stayed at my aunt's house so I could get ready without him seeing me in my gown. But I started to get nervous and couldn't sleep that night. I hated being away from him. So I went to our apartment just so I could give him a kiss good-night."

Her eyes glassed over as she wrung her hands together. I grabbed one and wrapped my fingers around it. Suddenly all I wanted was to help make her pain go away.

She smiled up at me and took a deep breath. "The lights were on in the living room when I pulled up, and I could see him inside with my best friend." The tears slipped over her lashes and disappeared into the dark fabric of her dress.

"I'm so sorry."

"He wasn't. They married six months later and even invited me to the wedding." She laughed sadly as she shook her head and more tears rolled over her cheeks. "I lost my friend, my fiancé, and my future all because I wanted a kiss good-night."

Her gaze fell to my lips and she whispered my name before pushing her mouth softly against mine.

CHAPTER Eighteen

SARAH

I WASN'T A FAN of getting dressed up when I didn't have to, but I didn't want to look like a bum next to Donna. She was always so pulled together. I wished my life were as simple as hers. I tried to push the thought of her being with E out of my mind.

I pulled on a pair of dark-wash skinny jeans with my brown suede boots, topping it off with a cream-colored sweater that fell off the shoulder. That was as fancy as I was going to get. I didn't know why we were even bothering. The guys wouldn't be with us tonight. I tried to push the thought of Derek in a strip club out of my mind.

"Why do you look so fucking worried?" He laughed and kissed me on the cheek.

I narrowed my eyes at him and put my hands on my hips. "Because you're going to have half-naked chicks all around you."

"And you're going out looking like that."

"What is that supposed to mean?"

He laughed and shook his head. "It means you look beautiful and every guy is going to be trying to get with you."

My heart melted a little and I couldn't help but smile at his being worried about me and not thinking about strippers. He was all I had in the world now, and I knew how unhealthy that was, but I couldn't handle being hurt any more. Couldn't handle being alone.

"We are just going to have a few drinks and talk about you guys. You have nothing to worry about." He pressed his lips against mine and turned to walk out the door.

I sighed as I made my way into the bathroom to look in the mirror. I was as good as I was going to get. I turned off the light and headed down the hall to Donna's room.

I knocked and there was no answer. I waited a few seconds before knocking harder as E's door opened and they both stepped into the hall.

"Oh . . . I thought you would be in your room getting ready." I tried not to look disappointed as my eyes met E's.

He quickly turned his attention back to Donna. "Have fun." He pressed his lips to her hair.

It shouldn't bother me. I had no right to care what was going on behind his closed door.

"You ready?" Donna asked as she made her way toward me. E was a few steps behind her.

"Yeah . . ." I refused to turn around and look at him as he went to the twins' room and banged on the door. The elevator dinged and Donna and I both stepped inside, leaning against the back wall. The door began to close and at the last second my eyes fell on his, as I was unable to stop myself.

Cass was in the lobby kissing Tucker good-bye. I wrapped my arms around her and squeezed tight. I needed to tell her everything that had been going on, but I couldn't do that with Donna around, and the only other person I could open up to was E, and I just couldn't.

I put my smile in place along with the walls that I used to keep people from seeing what was really going on inside me. This night was a celebration of Cass and Tucker's getting married and I wouldn't ruin it for my friend.

Tucker had a car waiting for us outside so we wouldn't need to bother with calling a cab and we could get around the city without his having to worry about Cass. We decided to head to Flower, an upscale bar just a few miles away.

The place was crowded but everyone was much calmer and more relaxed than at our usual haunts. We grabbed a table near the front window and ordered up a round of supergirlie drinks as Cass spilled the details of her time alone with Tucker. To hear how much love she had for him made my heart physically ache.

They had stayed at a swanky hotel about a half hour away called the Amore. Their suite was the size of a large apartment, with a hot tub in the bedroom. The walls were painted a deep royal blue with white slink curtains and bed linens. The paintings that lined the walls nearly stretched from floor to ceiling, and Tucker made sure the kitchen was stocked with all of Cass's favorite snacks and a bottle of fizzy, pink champagne.

"The whole world just flipped on its axis since I met him. I never knew what it felt like to be genuinely happy." Cass shrugged and Donna and I both oohed and aahed at her declarations of love.

I was surprised how Cass and I fell right back into conversation as if we hadn't spent months apart. We had talked constantly on the phone while we were both separately on the road, but it wasn't the same as having her by my side.

I started to warm up around Donna as well. She seemed like a nice person with a good heart, but I still wasn't convinced she was a good fit for E. He needed someone he could share his secrets with and who wouldn't run when he had one of his epic meltdowns. He carried a lot around inside him, and I wasn't convinced she could handle it.

I wondered if he had confided about his childhood with her, and the thought made me feel betrayed. I hated myself for wishing he couldn't share his past with others . . . but I did.

I tried to include her in the conversation and not cringe when I mentioned her and E.

"How long have you been together?" I asked, trying to sound cheery.

Donna's eyes went to Cass and back to me. "Not long. It's all kind of new." Donna smiled.

Cass looked at me with wide eyes and I knew we'd have to find a moment to steal away later. I had so much I needed to tell her. And so much I needed to get a firmer hold on myself.

CHAPTER Nineteen

ERIC

RAP MUSIC BLARED over the speakers as we made our way from the hotel to the dimly lit strip club. My head was swimming from everything that was going on. This was the last fucking thing I wanted to be doing, but this was about Tuck and I wasn't going to let my mood ruin his night.

Everything had been so clear to me before. I wanted Sarah. So why the fuck had Donna kissed me . . . and why had I so willingly kissed her back? Our drunken hookup had clearly been fueled by alcohol, but that kiss was something else. Passion and pain were in that kiss. There was definitely nothing friendly about it.

I needed a break from all of this.

We took our seats along the stage as Tuck ordered us a round of beers.

"What happened to your face, man?" Tuck asked Derek, and I laughed, clearing my throat to try to cover my reaction.

"Bar fight." Derek's eyes drifted to me.

I just shook my head, looking up the dancer on the stage. She was blond and curvy and her eyes were locked on mine as she walked around the pole and sank down to her knees. I grinned up at her as I relaxed back in my seat, my eyes looking over her tramp stamp as she spun around.

Our drinks arrived and I was thankful to have something to help cloud my conscience so I could feel a little less of everything.

"We should get you a lap dance," Terry called out to Tucker.

He shook his head. "I don't think my wife would like that." He grinned as he called her "wife" and I couldn't help but smile. Cass and I had had our issues in the past, but I loved her like a sister and I was glad that she had found her happy ending.

"Whipped already. That's why I stay single," Chris chimed in.

"Yeah, that's why," I spoke up.

He hit my chest with the back of his hand. "Bitches can't handle this."

I just shook my head and laughed as I drank my beer.

One became ten and I lost count as an endless parade of strippers took the stage. I wanted to go back to my room and pass out.

"You in the band, too?" a voice purred from beside me as she trailed her hand across my shoulders and walked to the front of me.

"Drummer." I nodded.

She straddled my legs and began to dance suggestively. "Little drummer boy."

"Nothing little about me, sweetheart." I smiled at her and she giggled. Her hands slid through my hair, pulling my head back as she pressed her body against mine. Her smile never reached her eyes, and it turned my stomach to have her grinding on me when I knew it wasn't what she wanted.

I grabbed her wrists and gently pulled them back so she wasn't touching me.

"You don't like it?" She stuck her lip out as if she were pouting.

"It's not you. My mind is . . . elsewhere." I grabbed a fifty from my wallet and gave it to her. I just wanted to nurse my beer and get this night over with as soon as possible.

She didn't look happy but she walked over to another patron and offered him a dance. I stared off at the flashing lights over the stage wondering what the girls were up to.

"What did you do?" Tuck asked as he sank down in the seat next to me. He was the only other guy not getting a private dance.

"I'm just not in the mood."

Tucker made a face as if I were fucking crazy and I just shook my head. "Only you can piss off a woman whose job it is to like you."

"It's a gift," I joked. "Nothing is right. Everything I touch I fuck up."

"Like Derek's face?" Tucker cocked his eyebrow, a smile playing on his lips.

"Among other things." I took another drink.

"Right." Tucker set his bottle down and spun it in his hand. "I know I was kind of a dick when you were trying to get with Sarah on tour. I just didn't want everything to get fucked-up for us."

"It doesn't really matter. I could never get her alone long enough to give us a chance. Now I can't even make things right. Derek won't let me near her." I nodded my head toward Derek, who was fully engrossed in the woman grinding against his crotch. "And now I've totally fucked up our friendship. I feel like I'm losing her completely . . . if I haven't already. Derek just doesn't deserve her."

"Agreed."

"Why does that fuckstick get the girl? When do I get my shot?"

"Why was it so hard for Cass to leave Jax? She's probably scared, man. You need to show her she deserves better, but she isn't going to make that decision until she is ready. You're asking for her to change her entire life and take a chance on the unknown."

"I get two weeks, Tuck. Two fucking weeks or I lose her for good."

"I'll see what I can do." Tucker stood, patting me on the shoulder as he went up to Chris and said something quietly to him. Chris looked over at me and back at Tuck before he nodded. Then he pulled his cell phone out of his pocket and walked toward the exit with his finger in his ear so he could hear.

I tapped my finger on the table to the sound of the drums in the song. Tucker came back a few minutes later and nodded as he sat down across from me.

"You want your chance? We'll keep that douche bag out here for a few more hours. The club closes at three."

"It doesn't matter. Things with Donna are weird now."

"Yeah, that's what Cass said on the phone. She is handling that. Just go hang out with her. Get your closure so you can stop with this brooding bullshit." He smiled as he peeled the label from his bottle.

"I owe you one, man." I stood, glancing around at the guys, who seemed oblivious to what I was doing. I slipped out of the club and hailed a taxi to take me back to the hotel.

I was nervous the entire trip back. I didn't want to put Sarah behind me, but I knew that was probably how this night would end.

I paid the cabdriver as we pulled up out front, and my eyes scanned the tall building. I didn't know if Sarah was already in her room, and I wasn't even sure she would answer if she was.

I rode up to our floor as my mind raced. I contemplated just going to my room and lying down, but as I passed by her door, I could hear her softly singing to herself. I couldn't help but smile as I stepped closer.

I knocked lightly and her voice abruptly cut off. I took a step back and waited for her to pull open the door.

She looked surprised as she scanned the hall to see if I was alone. "What are you doing here? I thought you guys were shuttin' down the club." Her lips quirked in a smile and I relaxed.

"Headache. I just needed to relax a little." I cocked my head to the side as I took in that she was wearing only an oversize T-shirt. My eyes rested on the thin, pink scar that was on the top of her thigh about the size of the scars that covered her arm, and my heart hurt. I knew I couldn't turn back now. I couldn't live with myself if she felt that being with Derek was her only option. I'd put everything on the line for her.

"Cass wasn't feeling well." We looked at each other for a moment. "I think Donna is up with her going over the scheduling."

"You want to hang out for a few?"

"Oh . . . I don't know if that is a good idea."

"I'd love to hear what you were singing."

Her cheeks turned pink and she smiled, embarrassed. "You heard that?"

"Was I not supposed to? You sing onstage in front of hundreds of people for a living."

"This was just . . . I was just trying to flesh out some lyrics. It's not really ready yet."

"Let's hear what you got. Maybe I can help." I took a step forward and she worried her lip but stepped back so I could enter.

I looked around the room that was identical to mine but flipped.

"You can"—she gestured toward the bed—"uh . . . sit if you want."

She grabbed a pair of shorts from her bag and went into the bathroom to pull them on. When she came back out, my eyes automatically went to her.

"Derek is going to freak if he comes back and you're in here."

"He won't be back for hours. The club doesn't close until three. If you want, we can go to my room. I have a bottle."

"Okay." We grabbed her lyrics and her guitar and snuck up the hall to my room.

She pulled open my fridge and grabbed the bottle of Jack.

"I stopped on the way home. I figured it would be a late night. I'll pour the shots. I want you to sing to me." I took the bottle from her hand. My fingers wrapped around hers.

"Okay." She was so much more timid than her normal self. She set her guitar down against the counter.

I grabbed two cups from the cupboard and filled them each with a double shot. Sarah came to my side with a paper in her hand, and I could see it vibrate slightly as her hand shook.

I grabbed her glass and held it out to her. "To good friends and good music." I held my glass in the air and she bumped hers against mine. We drank them down quickly and slammed our cups on the counter.

"All right." She cleared her throat and her eyes fell closed. She began to sing in a low, sad tone as if she were in pain.

The flames lick at my fingertips as I'm drawn to the fire,
I want to run but I'm consumed by the overwhelming
    desire,
To let you in and break apart these walls,
That contain me, don't blame me, I'm trying not to fall,
But it hurts to ignore it and it hurts to lie,
By myself in this bed when I'm starting to cry.

Her eyes rose to meet mine and I was speechless. It was as if she took the words directly from my heart.

"Did you write that . . . here?" What I was really asking was whom she was writing about.

She slowly nodded. Her face was nervous and unsure.

"It's perfect."

"Thanks." Her voice was quiet. "I'm not sure where to go from there. I'm kind of . . . stuck."

"You're not free . . ." I let my words trail off as I remembered her text message. I wanted to beg her to explain what it meant, but I knew she would close herself off again. "Would you like me to help you? We could figure it out together."

"Yeah . . . um . . . let me grab my guitar."

I poured us each another drink and carried them toward the main area of the room. Sarah sat down on the bed, her legs folded in front of her and her acoustic guitar on her lap. She strummed a few chords as I sat down next to her, my body angled toward her.

"Thanks." She took the glass from my hand and her eyes stayed on me as she drank it back. I did the same and took our cups, setting them on the nightstand.

"I like that," I said as she strummed. I watched her mouth as she slowly began to sing. Her voice was unbelievable. "Let's work on a chorus." I grabbed the paper and her pen and began to jot a few lines down.

At night when I close my eyes, I think of you in another life,
No longer hiding
What I've been fighting

We took turns strumming the guitar and writing. Sarah loosened up and was starting to act like her old self from the tour. She was focusing on getting out her feelings, and nothing but honesty was in her lyrics.

"Why are you not a singer?" she asked as she poured us another drink and my eyes scanned her soft legs from the bed.

"That's for the pretty people," I joked.

She shot me a flirtatious glance. "You're pretty." She sat down next to me, her bare thigh against my jeans.

"I'm not sure if I should be flattered or insulted." I took my glass and held it in the air. "What to?"

"To this . . . this is nice . . . ," she sighed.

"To what?" I asked as my eyes searched hers.

"This . . . us."

"To us. That's better." I drank down my shot.

She smiled and tossed hers back. "You really are more than just a pretty face."

That caused me to laugh loudly and I bumped her with my shoulder, but she winced in pain.

"What? What happened?"

"Nothing."

"Sarah . . ." I leaned away a few inches so I could pull up her short sleeve over her shoulder. A purpling bruise marred her creamy skin.

"What happened?" The playfulness had left my tone. "Did he do this?"

"No. Jesus, E. He doesn't hit me." She shook her head and looked down at her lap. "I was fucked-up the other night. I couldn't snap out of it. I tripped going into the bathroom."

"When you texted me and I didn't answer."

She slowly nodded and I felt like such an asshole. I ran my hand through my hair as I turned more toward her, our bodies danger- ously close. I reached out, my eyes on hers as I took my finger and slowly pushed up the leg of her shorts to expose the barely healed scar.

"And what about this?"

She pushed her shorts back down and her eyes watered over. She glanced toward the door as if she was contemplating running.

"You don't have to hide from me, Sarah. You never did before, and you don't have to now."

"That's from a long time ago." She wiped at a tear as she strug- gled not to break down.

"Please don't ever do that to yourself again. Please . . ." Her eyes met mine and my heart stopped.

"Okay," she whispered. Her bottom lip quivered and I knew she was trying so hard to be strong.

I reached out and ran my thumb over her lip and her breathing stuttered. I wanted to lean over and kiss her, but I forced myself not to. I would be whatever she wanted me to be for her, as long as she didn't shut me out.

"Sarah, I want to know what is hurting you. Why you are hurting yourself."

"I want to tell you. . . ."

"You can tell me anything." I ran my thumb over the back of her hand and she began to relax a little. She closed her eyes, breathed in deeply, and began to speak in a quiet, shaky voice.

"I never really felt safe at home after my mom married Phil. He would always make inappropriate comments, hug me just a little too long. I didn't know what to do. He was my stepfather."

My mind raced as Sarah began to tell me everything she'd endured as a child. Part of me had always suspected abuse given the few details she'd let slip about her past and the way she behaved around Derek, but never to this magnitude. It made perfect sense now why she reacted the way she did to Derek's behavior. I cringed as I thought of the first time she was alone with me in my room and I'd wanted her so badly. She was probably terrified of me.

"I will fucking kill him." I knew it wasn't what she needed right now, but I couldn't fathom that no one had tried to protect her.

"It's over, E. He can't hurt me anymore."

"But he *is* still hurting you. Everything you do is a direct result of your past, of what happened to you."

"It doesn't matter anymore."

"Where is he?" I couldn't hide my anger and I knew I was squeezing her fingers too tightly.

"I don't know. I haven't spoken to my mother in years . . . or my sister."

"Do you think they are still together?"

"I don't know. Even if they aren't, I don't think I could ever go back there. When I left . . . I left for good. I never looked back.

I cut all my ties to my old life, cut everyone out completely and just fled. . . . I never wanted to be reminded of him in any way again. . . ."

"You don't have to." Her eyes met mine for a brief second, and I knew she understood just how far I was willing to go to protect her.

"People always talk about a house with a white picket fence." She shook her head. "We hid a lot of secrets behind that fence."

"Why didn't you tell someone?"

"Who would I tell?" Anger flashed in her eyes. "My mother knew I hated Phil. I wanted them to break up from day one. I doubt she would have even believed me."

"I believe you."

"You're different."

"I've been called worse," I said with a laugh, and she smiled. It was a small victory and I hated that she was with someone who didn't give a damn about her feelings. "Why haven't you told Derek?"

"Embarrassed, I guess. Or maybe just scared. Scared he'd freak out, not be able to handle it." She was fighting back tears now. "I'm just . . . I'm scared to be left alone."

Again I had that nagging thought that Sarah would hate me for keeping the truth about Derek from her, but I couldn't hurt her any more. Not now. I just couldn't, even though I knew it was only a matter of time before she caught him in the act again.

"Have you ever thought about finding your real dad?" I didn't want to press her, but there had to be someone she could turn to.

Derek obviously wasn't that person, and I knew once she left here with him, I'd probably never see her again.

"He's been gone since I was six, E. If my mom couldn't find him, he doesn't want to be found."

"Whatever happened between him and your mom is between them. You can still have a relationship with him."

"Oh, like your relationship with *your* dad?"

"Things with my dad are different, Sarah. He blames me for my brother's death and used me as a punching bag." It wasn't fair to ask her to do something that I wasn't willing to do myself, and I honestly am scared that he won't want to see me. It is hard to put yourself out there for someone and be rejected.

"I know. I'm sorry. I'm just saying time can change things. You never know."

"Maybe you're right. If I could talk to him man-to-man, I might be able to put some of this shit behind me. You could do the same, you know?" The thought of being able to move past what had happened seemed like a dream. My father and I couldn't make up the years we lost, but it would be nice to have a family again.

She sighed loudly as hers eyes darted everywhere but to mine. "He left with the neighbor lady and never looked back. It doesn't even matter. I have Derek."

I struggled against asking again why she was telling me all of her secrets and not him, but I didn't want to hurt her more.

"If he is what makes you happy, then I am happy for you, Sarah." I couldn't bring myself to let go of her hand even though the contact was becoming almost painful. "But I think you should tell him about what you went through."

"I can't. He wouldn't understand."

"If he loves you, he would."

She looked over at me again and I knew she could see what I was feeling written all over my face.

CHAPTER

Twenty

SARAH

I HAD THOUGHT ABOUT telling Derek about my childhood a million times, but I always just assumed it would cause him to run. I wanted to believe that it would just be too much for him to handle, but deep down I often wondered if he did really love me. It scared the shit out of me that I was able to open up to E, something I could never do with Derek. E said himself if Derek loved me, he would react the same way E had, and I wanted to know how much E really cared for me. He didn't judge me, didn't try to pull away. He just listened.

"You understand . . ." An unasked question was in my words.

E nodded, his free hand running over my cheek and trailing over my jaw. "I do."

My heart thudded in my chest as the pad of his thumb ran over my lower lip. I felt my body leaning toward him as his gaze dipped to my mouth and back to my eyes. He pressed his forehead against mine, his eyes falling closed as mine did.

I felt emotionally exhausted. Spilling my secrets had been too much. "What are you thinking?" I whispered.

"You don't want to know." He laughed and shook his head.

I smacked him on the arm and pulled back from him. "You are such a perv."

"I don't get many complaints," he joked, and suddenly I remembered. He was with Donna. All of a sudden, I'd never felt so exposed to anyone.

I was struggling not to let myself give in to what I was feeling. Every time he touched me, his fingers brushed against me, it ignited a fire inside me that spread clear down to my toes. I had never felt that with anyone before; my fear and guilt from my past had usually drowned out any other feelings for anyone.

"I've missed you." The confession slipped out as I stared into his sad blue eyes. The corner of his mouth pulled into a smile, revealing one of his dimples. His arms slipped around my neck and he pulled me to him. I didn't try to pull away.

"Is this okay?" he whispered into my hair as he hugged me. I could only nod because the feeling of him pressed against my body was overwhelming. I spread my fingers out over his sides, sighing as my palms flattened on the straining muscles of his back. "You have no idea how much I missed you, Sarah. So much."

I closed my eyes and inhaled the unmistakable scent of E, Polo Sport and whiskey, as his chest rose and fell quickly against mine. I could feel his heart hammering in his chest in time with mine.

"Do you know how hard it is to stay away from you? I've been dying to pull you into my arms since the wedding." His voice broke as he whispered his confession.

"You can't say things like that." The guilt of what I was feeling was killing me inside, but I didn't have the strength to pull back from him. For a brief moment I was released from my cage.

"I'm sorry." His lips moved against my cheek. He slowly pulled his body away from mine, and I immediately regretted what I'd said.

Without thinking I put my leg over his lap so I was straddling him. He groaned at the more intimate contact. I rested my forehead on his and my mouth fell open as my breathing increased. He never made a move to kiss me, but somehow this felt more intimate.

We sat perfectly still like this, enjoying the high of being so close. I could feel how much he wanted me as he pressed against my center. I brought my hands to his chest and placed my hand over his heart as it thumped against my fingertips. His hands moved up my thighs and the tips of his fingers slipped just under the edge of my shorts and over the thin scar I had put there.

"Sarah . . . ," he growled, and I felt it through every inch of my body. I slowly opened my eyes, my breathing embarrassingly loud in the quiet room. "If you keep panting like that, I'm not going to be able to keep my hands off you."

I looked into Eric's eyes. The intensity of his gaze made me realize that I was getting in too deep. "I shouldn't be here."

His fingers slid to my hips and he held me firmly against him. My body sagged and my lips brushed over his as he spoke. "Stay with me. Just let me hold you."

"You know I can't."

"Just for a little while longer."

I moved my face so we were cheek to cheek and his heavy breaths blew across my ear.

The phone in the room began to ring and E's fingers slid into my hair.

"Ignore it," he panted.

I let my mouth fall open slightly, wishing that I could let go and take what I wanted.

Eventually, the noise stopped and E's fingers continued to stroke my hair. "I want you." His whispered confessions sounded deafening in the quiet space.

"E . . . don't do that." I didn't want more guilt to carry around with me. I was already carrying more than most could handle. I was buckling under the weight.

"I won't ever cross that line if that's what you want from me. This is enough."

I nodded, unable to respond as a lump formed in my throat. I could just be friends with E. It was better than the alternative, not having him in my life.

The phone rang again and his body grew rigid as he stared at me with wanting and sadness in his eyes.

"It could be important," he groaned.

I only nodded, unable to form any coherent words. I pulled my body from his, and I was overcome with embarrassment and regret the moment we broke contact. I was going to be sick. What had I done? I had let E get close to me and Derek would never forgive me.

"What?" E asked angrily as he answered the phone. His eyes flicked to me and he rubbed his hand over his forehead. "How long?" After a pause he added, "Thanks, man." Before he hung up the phone, his eyes danced over my body.

"What is it?" I asked, registering the sadness in his eyes.

"They guys are on their way back. . . ."

"Oh." I was suddenly feeling overwhelmed with panic. "I should . . . I should go." My eyes searched the room, unsure of what had come over me.

"You don't have to." He took a step in front of me, his hands taking mine. I stared down at where he touched me and slowly looked up to meet his gaze.

"E . . ." There were no words. I was a horrible human

being. E and Derek both deserved better than what I was giving them right now—I was a shitty girlfriend to Derek and a shitty friend to E. I deserved to be alone and ashamed.

He let go of my hands and took a step back, the look of lust replaced with a hardened mask as the muscles in his jaw flexed under his skin.

I could only nod once at him and hurried out of the room and down the hall to mine.

My mind was racing when I got inside. Part of me was relieved Derek hadn't beat me back and part of me overwhelmed with guilt for what I had just done. While technically my actions had stayed chaste, I knew that my heart wasn't being faithful.

I curled up the center of the bed, my fingers running over the scar on my thigh that still tingled from E's touch. My thoughts were consumed by him and I hated myself the more my heart raced. I wanted to run back to him and let whatever happened happen, but instead I lay frozen in the deafening silence of my room.

It felt like hours as the minutes ticked by as I hummed "Free Bird," trying desperately to escape into my mind and not have to face Derek. Finally, I heard the handle of the door move and the lock click free from the frame. I sat up, staring at the door as I held my breath. Tucker stepped inside with Derek's arm pulled around his neck. They stumbled toward me, Derek's eyes unfocused.

"Does this belong to you?" Tucker asked with a smirk. Something in his tone made me uncertain if he knew where I had just been. I just looked at him, the question written all over my face. He winked and unlooped Derek's body from his. "Well, I'll just leave him here." Derek twisted and fell back onto the bed beside me.

Tucker turned and walked back toward the door.

"Thank you," I called after him.

He turned back with a smile. "That's what friends are for." The door closed behind him and I let go of the breath I had been holding as I looked down at Derek.

"Who was that boy?" Phil screamed, and spittle flew from his mouth as the vein in his neck pulsed under his weathered flesh.

"He was just walking me home. He's just a friend." I tried to keep my voice even, but as Phil stepped toward me, I flinched and covered my face with my hands, hoping that if I couldn't see him, he would disappear. I wasn't that lucky. I was never lucky.

"If I catch him around you again, you're grounded."

"That's not fair! He's just a friend and you know I don't have many."

"You want me to tell your mother that you're out acting like a slut?" he bit out angrily and stepped closer.

"You can't keep me locked away like a prisoner."

"*We can and we will. You live under my roof and what I say goes.*"

"*This roof was paid for by my father,*" I snapped. I hated Phil with every fiber of my being.

"*You want to live with your father? Be my guest. Leave.*"

It killed me inside when I thought about my dad. I had no idea where he was, but anywhere would be better than here. "*Maybe I will.*"

"*If you do, don't you ever come back, do you understand me?*"

CHAPTER Twenty-One

ERIC

LAY AWAKE FOR hours as I thought about Sarah. I wanted so desperately for her to stay with me. It was almost worse that I was finally able to touch her and have her want this as badly as I did, only to have her walk out of the door . . . for *him*.

I was sickened as I thought of him being able to sleep beside her, to hold her, and I was forced to pretend that I wasn't feeling as if my entire world were imploding.

I wanted her and wanted to forget her at the same time. Her song lyrics played over and over in my head, torturing me. Karma was perpetually punishing me for not saving my brother from that car. Everything in my life fell apart after that day and I had stopped caring.

"I just spent three hours on the phone with your coach."

I sat up on my bed and pulled off my headphones, trying to hide that I was high from my dad.

"You have screwed up your entire life. I hope you're happy."

I rolled my eyes and lay back against my pillow. "Yeah, I'm fucking ecstatic."

"What the hell did you just say to me, boy?" he yelled, and my mother was at his side, latching onto his arm to hold him in place.

I pushed to my feet, puffing out my own chest to meet his as I looked him in the eye. "You don't scare me, old man. You're just jealous I was better than you ever were."

"Better? You got kicked off the damn team! You won't ever get into college now."

"At least I made the team," I smirked, feeling no fear.

"Eric! Don't you dare talk to your father that way!" my mother screamed, and my father's fist connected with the side of my face.

I stumbled, but I was younger and stronger. I took another step closer to him so we were chest to chest. "You want to kick my ass? Take another swing, asshole. I will lay you out."

His eyes widened and he shoved against my chest. I wrapped an arm around his and shoved back, sending us tumbling to the floor. My mom screamed and jumped out of the way as we rolled around together exchanging blows. By the time she got us separated, my lip was bloodied and my dad's eye was swelling and turning purple. I smiled, happy he would finally wear a badge of abuse from me.

"Eric, look what you did!" My mom grabbed his face and inspected the damage.

I touched my lip, pulling back my fingers and examining the smeared blood. "Yeah, it's all my fault. It's always my fault."

"I want you out of my house," my dad shouted, struggling to catch his breath.

"It's my house, too," I yelled back as my eyes met my mother's, but she looked to the ground and all I could do was nod.

My dad took a step closer to me, his cold eyes locked onto mine. "The wrong son died that day."

It hurt worse than any physical blow, and I almost buckled at the pain that ripped through my heart. It was one thing to think it about myself, but to hear my own father say it killed me inside.

"Fuck you both," I spat angrily as I shoved by him and out the door.

I gave up on trying to get some sleep as the sun rose outside my window. I moved around my room, getting ready for the day. I felt empty and spinning out of control. I wanted to see her, to look her in the eye and know that last night had really happened. That the look in her eyes and the love in her voice as she sang to me were real.

I had no reason to knock on her door and it would only raise suspicion in Derek, not that I would mind seeing the look on his face as I pulled Sarah into my arms and pressed my lips against hers.

I stepped out of my hotel room and walked down the hallway, feeling as if I were walking to my execution. I glanced to her door, knowing she was just on the other side, curled up in his arms. I forced my feet to keep moving until I reached Donna's door.

She answered after my second knock, wearing a silky, pink robe that fell midthigh. She stepped back to let me in without saying a word, her smile faltering as she saw my expression. I didn't know what I was doing here. Given the way everything had changed between Donna and me, I knew I couldn't talk to her about Sarah, but I couldn't be alone, either. I didn't trust myself.

"What's wrong?" She closed the door and wrapped her arms around her waist.

"I think I need to leave, get away for a while." I leaned back against the kitchen counter as I stared at the floor between us. She took a step closer but stopped as she looked me over.

"Is this because of me?"

"No." I shook my head. "This is because of me. I just need to spend some time . . . alone." All I did was fuck up everyone's life that I came in contact with. I was meant to be on my own.

She nodded, but didn't respond.

"I feel like I'm losing myself."

"E . . . I'm sorry I kissed you. I know it wasn't the right thing to do. I'm your manager, your friend . . . I shouldn't let things get so complicated."

I took a step forward and wrapped my arms around her body. "Don't. You don't need to apologize." I rested my chin on top of her head as I closed my eyes. "You are one of my closest friends." I pulled back, placing a hand on either side of her face as I looked her in the eye. "I can't lose you." I pressed my lips to her forehead as she sighed, and her hands came up to wrap around mine.

"I'm not going anywhere, E. And neither are you. I won't let you leave. You don't run away from your problems."

I smiled down at her. I wanted to tell her how wrong she was. Running is exactly what I did. I've been running most of my life.

"It's gotten too hard." I shook my head.

"That's what she said." A proud smile spread across her face.

I let out a genuine laugh as I pulled her in for another hug, rubbing my hand over her back. "That is why I love you." My laugh died in my throat as her body stiffened from my words. I silently cursed myself as I gave her a squeeze and took a step back. I shouldn't have used that word with Donna, especially given what I meant by it. I knew her trust issues ran deep, and I was only going to make things between us more complicated. I loved her as a friend, deeply, but that would never be what she needed or wanted.

I ran my hand over my messy hair as I watched her. "Let's get out of this hotel and go do something normal."

Her smile returned and she nodded before slipping into her bathroom to change her clothes. I sat on the edge of her bed, leaning on my knees as I waited for her to come out.

She emerged a few minutes later in jeans and a white tank top, her hair pulled back in a ponytail. "Where are we going?" she asked with a smile.

"Wherever you want." I pushed to my feet and walked over to the door, opening it for her. She stepped out and stopped as our eyes landed on Terry and Chris, who were in the hall chatting animatedly about the strippers from last night.

"Where are you two off to?" Chris asked playfully. I rolled my eyes and looked to Donna.

"Um . . . I was thinking about the zoo." She glanced back at me to see if I approved.

"Sounds good to me." I nodded at Terry as I continued by toward the elevator with Donna in front of me.

"Enjoy your date," Terry called after us, and I stuck my middle finger in the air as the elevator doors opened and we slipped inside.

I leaned against the back wall as I shoved my hands in my pockets.

"I didn't think it was a date," she said nervously.

I couldn't help but smile. "Call it what you want. Those guys are just assholes. Don't let them get to you." The doors opened and we stepped out into the lobby. I placed my arm over her shoulders as we stepped out into the entirely too bright world. I flagged down a cab that quickly pulled along the curb for us. I opened the door and made a sweeping gesture for her to get in.

"Lockwood Zoo," I told the cabdriver as he pulled out into traffic as I relaxed against the seat.

"You have fun last night?" Donna asked, and I could feel her eyes on me.

I nodded and looked out the window as I cleared my throat. I didn't want to talk about last night, about how I had managed to spend some alone time with Sarah. It just didn't feel right to bring it up to her anymore, and it was too painful to think about. The line between friendship and relationship had become blurry with Donna. I knew she was trusting me more, but my heart belonged to only one person.

"You?" I asked, still not looking at her.

"It was fun. Nice to spend some time without a bunch of drunk guys around." She giggled.

"That what I am to you?" I put my hand over my heart, pretending to be offended.

"You know what I mean." She rolled her eyes.

"Yeah, I get it. That's why I want to get away. Step outside this box we live in."

"You ever think of what you would be doing if you weren't in the band?"

"I, uh . . . I think I would have made a good soldier." I glanced over at Donna, whose mouth was open. "What? You don't think I could do it?"

"I can't picture you taking orders from anyone." She shook her head, clearly amused.

"You want to do what?" My father was clearly not amused.

"The army would be good for me. There is nothing wrong with fighting for your country."

"How do expect to do that, Eric? You think they let any screwup with a record in?" He flipped the page of his newspaper, not even bothering to look up at me.

"I can explain what happened. I'm a minor. In a few months I'll be an adult and I can go off to basic. It would get me out of here."

I hated how much it bothered me that they wanted me gone, but I hoped it would be a good selling point.

"You would just screw that up, too. The army is for men, not boys."

"Maybe if my father took the time to teach me how to be a man, I wouldn't be such a fucking disappointment!" The air left my lungs as my father's eyes locked on to mine.

"What did you say to me? You think you can screw up your life and blame it on me?" He pushed up from his chair, the newspaper falling to the ground. I widened my stance and braced myself for the inevitable blow to come. It was too late to back down now.

"Not everything is my fault." I yelled, hoping my voice sounded confident. "I want to be a good person. If I could join, I could make you proud."

"It's too late for that," he said with a sneer and turned to leave me standing alone, ready for a fight.

I shook the memory from my mind and tucked my arm behind my head as my lack of sleep began to hit me. "Yeah, I guess I would have a little trouble with that." I loved how easy our conversations were. I didn't have to try with Donna, we could just hang out, and we got each other.

We pulled into the zoo parking lot and I thanked the driver and paid him the fare. I slipped out onto the sidewalk and stretched as I waited for Donna to join me.

"I haven't been to a zoo in years." She was beaming from ear to ear as her eyes danced over the entrance.

"I can't ever remember being to one." I pushed the thought of my childhood into the back of my mind.

"Even better. New memories." She looped her arm in mine and pulled me toward the ticket counter.

We made our way down the bamboo-lined paths as I held her hand in mine.

"'They are pink because of what they eat,'" Donna said, reading the sign to the flamingo exhibit. "So glad humans aren't that way."

I pulled her into my side and lightly kissed the top of her head. "You'd be adorable pink," I joked, and she rolled her eyes. The carefree Donna that usually only emerged when she had a few drinks was out to play, and I loved that she felt so comfortable around me right now. Everything suddenly felt so normal, for the first time since . . . since I could remember.

"Be thankful. I don't even want to think of what color you would be because you're so full of shit," she joked.

I hugged her tightly into my side as I laughed. "Jesus, you've been hanging around the guys too long."

"It's nice being just the two of us."

I was taken aback by her comment but it was the truth. It was easier. Being around her took away the stress that had been piling up since Sarah had showed up at the wedding.

As we made our way to the macaws, she laughed as I flapped my arms trying to get them to mimic my movements. "You don't strike me as a bird guy."

"No? I could be a bird guy," I said as I looked over at her, unable to hide my content smile. Donna was like a bird. She was quick to take off if anyone got too close. Everything was a danger to her, but for some reason she trusted me and I didn't take that lightly.

CHAPTER

Twenty-Two

SARAH

I COULDN'T EAT AS I stared across the table at the twins. Derek was beside me, his hand resting on my thigh. I wanted to move away from him but I already felt guilty enough. I tried to convince myself that all I had done was hug E, but I knew it was more than that, at least to me.

"What do you want to do today, babe?" Derek asked.

All eyes fell to me as I dropped a cherry tomato back on my plate and shrugged. My eyes danced over the twins and I didn't like the way they were looking at me, so I dropped my gaze to my plate.

"I heard there was a badass movie that just came out. Zombie something or some shit." Terry reached across the table and grabbed my pickle, shoving the whole damn thing in his mouth.

"Why don't you just shoot me instead," I grumbled.

"Great idea! Paintball!" Chris yelled, and Derek laughed.

All I wanted to know was were E had gone with Donna. It was killing me to think he was out somewhere on a date after what had happened last night. I knew that made me a hypocrite, but it hurt just the same.

"The zoo," Terry said. His eyes met mine and he gave a small nod. Could he have known I was wondering where E was? It was as if he were reading my thoughts, which hardly seemed possible when none of these guys had thoughts of their own.

"Maybe I should just stay in and write." I suddenly remembered that I had left my song and guitar in E's room. The thought of having to face him again thrilled and terrified me. I entertained the idea of just letting him keep it. I could use a new guitar. Mine was old.

"How is it possible for you to be this boring?" Chris asked with a straight face.

I picked up the cherry tomato and tossed it at his head. My insides were tied in knots and it was almost painful to hold a normal conversation. Derek leaned back and put his arm across the seat behind me.

"Maybe we *should* stay in." He leaned in, rubbing his nose against my cheek as his other hand crept up my thigh, and I knew his hand was only a thin piece of fabric from my newest scar, on my leg. It angered me that he had never questioned how it had gotten there. Maybe he knew, maybe he just didn't care.

"How far is the zoo?" As soon as the question left my lips, the twins smirked and I felt ashamed.

"I'll call Tuck," Chris said as he leaned to his side and pulled his cell from his pocket.

Ten minutes later we were in separate cabs and on our way. Derek was still running his hands over me as much as possible, despite that Terry was sitting on the other side of me. He glanced down at Derek's hand on my leg.

"Don't let me stop you, you fucking perv."

Derek groaned and relaxed in his seat and I finally let the tension leave my muscles. How was Derek so oblivious to my aversion to being touched?

The cab ride couldn't be over fast enough. I wasn't even sure E was at the zoo, but anything would be a welcome distraction from all of this. My skin felt as if it were crawling and I forced the thought of releasing my pain from my mind.

As we pulled up out front, we all got out of our cabs. Cass made her way to my side and we headed over to the ticket counter.

It was unbearably hot out, but the bamboo that lined the paths offered enough shade to keep us all from passing out.

"I want to see the monkeys." Cass was excited and tugging on Tuck's arm.

"We brought the monkeys with us," I joked, and rolled my eyes as Chris grabbed his crotch.

Tucker smiled down at Cass, his fingers trailing over her jaw as he kissed her on the lips.

My heart sank. I stared off at the animal enclosures, feeling that in this moment I could relate to them much better than I could to my best friend.

"I miss not having you around," Cass said as the guys walked off a few feet and we wandered toward the spider monkey enclosure.

"Maybe we will tour together again." I shrugged.

"You think Derek would be okay with that?" Cass cocked her eyebrow.

I turned toward the animals. "Who knows?" My voice trailed off and Cass didn't press the issue.

"You want a snow cone?" Derek asked, and I nodded. He pulled his wallet from his pocket as he strolled over to the Snack Barn. I watched a woman pull her son to her side as she eyed Derek's tattoos.

"He seems to be playing nice," Cass's voice broke through my thoughts.

"Too little too late," I sighed, but immediately felt like an asshole. "I'm glad he is trying."

She nodded but didn't reply as Tuck put his arms around her waist from behind and whispered something in her ear. She nodded and he kissed her on the cheek before following after Derek.

"I miss this. Ever since the tour ended, things have been so . . . different."

"You missing some of us more than others?" Cass's eyebrow was cocked.

I shook my head with a laugh. "I don't know what you're talking about."

"You know what is amazing about you?" I honestly had no clue. "When I needed someone to talk to about . . . the past, you went out of your way to become my friend and to help me find a way to work through everything I was feeling. Without writing, I don't know what I would do."

"I am pretty awesome, aren't I?" I laughed.

Cass smiled, shaking her head. "You're an awesome friend. I want to be able to be there for you, too. You can talk to me about . . . anything that is going on, ya know?"

"Are we going to talk about periods and braid each other's hair?" I joked.

Cass made a face. "Don't act like you don't like doing my hair," she shot back playfully. "And as for the period thing . . . I kind of haven't had mine for a while."

"What? How long is a while?"

"You can't say anything until I am sure everything is okay. After everything that happened before . . ." She looked to the ground.

"How long?"

"It's been a month. I was freaked out. I wouldn't even take a test for the longest time because I was scared."

"But you took one? What did it say?" I was practically bouncing up and down.

Cass placed her finger over her lips to remind me to be quiet. She leaned in and her lips quirked into a smile. "It was positive."

I squealed and she smacked my arm. "Sorry! I can't help it. A little baby? I am so happy for you guys."

"You are the only one who knows for now. I want to make sure everything is all right before I say anything. I'm not sure Tucker could handle another loss."

"I promise I won't say anything, but you need to tell him soon, Cass. If something happened, he needs to be there for you."

"I will. I am just trying to find the right moment. Now you know my secret, so spill yours."

"I just don't know where to even begin. Everything is a mess. Derek is being amazing to me and we are finally in a good place."

"But?"

"But I . . . I think I'm falling for E." I worried my lip as I waited for her to tell me I was a bad person, but I knew she wouldn't. Cass never judged because she knew what it was like to be looked down on just because of where she came from. She knew what it was like to feel broken, torn, confused.

"I was there. I get it. You can't help who you have feelings for, but you need to decide who it is you want. Take it from me. You don't want things to blow up in your face, and it is no secret the way you guys look at each other. If we can see it, so can Derek." Cass leaned against the fencing around the animal cage.

Derek and Tuck made their way back over to us with snow cones in hand.

"Thank you." I took a cone from Derek's hand and he leaned in, giving me a quick kiss, leaving the lingering taste of blueberries on my lips.

"You taste better than the snow cone," he whispered against my lips.

CHAPTER

Twenty-Three

ERIC

DONNA HAD SOMEHOW succeeded in keeping my mind off Sarah for the most part. Usually the only activity that could keep my mind off the heavy stuff was performing with the band. I missed the stage and couldn't wait to get up there again. The loud music drowned out my thoughts, and the longer we stayed off tour, the deeper I slipped back into my old self, unable to pull my thoughts from my past.

"Oh my God! Are you Tucker White?" I heard a female call from the next path over. I grabbed Donna's hand and pulled her around the corner, my throat suddenly closing as I watched Derek kiss Sarah.

Cass's eyes found mine and regret washed over her face as Tucker signed a piece of paper for the teenage girl in front of him.

"Hey," Donna called out, and everyone turned to us. Donna held my hand tightly and stepped toward them, forcing me to go along.

"What the hell are you guys doing here?" I asked, trying not to sound irritated.

Chris pointed to Terry, who held up his hands in mock surrender and shook his head. I could only nod and run my free hand through my hair angrily.

My whole body ached as I forced myself not to go to Sarah and pull her away from Derek. I wanted to press my lips against hers so hard she forgot her own name. I could see her struggle to keep a smile on her face and it killed me inside.

"Where to?" Cass asked as she turned to Tucker.

He looked to me and I gave a quick nod, letting him know I was okay. "That way." He pointed to a path off to the left that had a sign reading ELEPHANTS at the entrance. We all began to walk as I let Donna's fingers slip from mine. It didn't feel right holding on to her and wishing it were someone else.

A woman was standing on a crate just outside the elephant enclosure, and a crowd had gathered around her in a semicircle as she spouted off facts. We all gathered close and Sarah's body was in front of mine. I stepped up beside her, Derek on her left and Donna on my right. A fucking love triangle.

I didn't take in anything that the woman said as I relived the night before over and over in my head. I felt Sarah's eyes on me and I suppressed a smile. Her eyes went forward and the back of her hand brushed against mine. I looped my pinkie in hers and tried my damnedest to focus ahead. I knew it was wrong and I would only end up hurting her, but I couldn't resist. If she was smart, she would pull away, but she didn't and I knew she was feeling the electricity that shot between us where our bodies connected. If anyone saw us, there would be no stopping the fight that would ensue, but I didn't give a fuck. I couldn't see anything but Sarah anymore.

I couldn't get enough of her. Every touch, every glance, was a high that I never wanted to come down from. My fingers brushed along her hip as we watched the macaws flap their wings and spout random phrases. Her chest brushed against my back as we looked in at the Galápagos tortoises. Her eyes locked onto my lips as we stood in front of the giraffe enclosure, and I closed my eyes as I pictured her body straddling mine as her sweet breath blew over my mouth. I opened my eyes and her chest was rising and falling quickly as her tongue ran over her lower lip. She was thinking the same thing I was. I was dying to get her alone, even for a second, so I could touch her. When we stood in front of the lion exhibit, I finally saw my chance.

"You want to ride the train?" I asked Donna, glancing over her shoulder to Sarah.

"Yeah, sounds fun." Donna smiled and I put my arm around her waist as we walked toward the small station. I leaned over the railing as we waited for the next ride, hating where my head was going. I didn't want to share Sarah, I didn't want to be her second choice, but my body wouldn't let me say no to her. The heartbreak I was going to suffer from this would kill me, but I welcomed death if I got to spend even another minute alone with Sarah.

The train pulled under the small wooden roof and we all filed into our seats. I walked by Sarah and Derek, my eyes on the ground as I guided Donna into the row directly behind them.

We pulled out and Sarah's hair blew back toward me, the smell of her fruity shampoo in the air. I stared out the side as we wound our way around the zoo and finally came up on the tunnel that ran behind the lion cages. My heart pounded in my chest as I watched the engine disappear into the blackness. As soon as our car was in the dark I leaned forward, sliding my hand along Sarah's neck and turning her head so I could press my mouth against her cheek. Her quiet gasp was swallowed by the echoing of the train engine off the tunnel walls.

Even with everyone else around us, it felt as if we were in our own private world. My fingers slid down over her throat before I shoved myself back against my seat and we were thrust into daylight once again. I could still feel the rhythm of her heartbeat in my fingertips, like a beat to a song that was only ours.

There was no more fighting it. I wanted her more than I wanted my next breath, and I couldn't stay away even if it slowly killed me inside. It was worth the pain to be able to be close to her.

I couldn't wipe the smile off my face for the rest of our time at the zoo. When we finally left and decided to go out to get dinner, I was even making small talk with Derek, even though it turned my stomach to see him sitting next to her. I understood why he would want me to stay away. She was irresistible and he never deserved her. No one did.

I pressed my foot against hers as I sat across from her at the table, craving to be closer to her. Derek rambled on and on about my missing out at the strip club last night, and I couldn't help but shake my head. Not only was he pissing off Sarah, but he couldn't imagine how great a time I had without them. My feelings were tearing me in two—my heart went out to Sarah, but selfishly I relished every second that Derek was digging himself deeper into a hole.

I dipped a fry in mayonnaise and shoved it in my mouth as I absentmindedly began to hum the song we were making together last night. I tried not to be affected by her knowing smile but my heart stuttered.

"I like that," Donna said as she stole one of my fries. "That a new song?"

I shook my head and took a drink of my soda. "Just something stuck in my head." I glanced up as I grabbed another fry.

"Who is looking for a little fun tonight?" Terry asked as he rubbed his hands together. The women collectively groaned in disgust and I laughed. "That's not what I meant." He shook his head as we all waited for him to elaborate. "Beatfest is tonight and it is only about an hour from here. I have been looking forward to this all week."

"This is going to be epic." Tucker crumbled up his napkin and tossed it on his plate.

Cass shrugged as her eyes wandered around the table.

"I'm up for it," I added as I finished my burger, and Sarah's foot moved against mine.

"I'll hook up transportation. Donna, you think we could get a limo on this short notice?" Tuck asked as the waitress came over and dropped off the check.

"It shouldn't be that hard," Donna spoke up.

"That's what she said!" Cass laughed, and I tossed a fry at her and shook my head.

CHAPTER

Twenty-Four

SARAH

WE RUSHED BACK to the hotel so we could get ready for the festival. I was excited to dress up in some of my concert gear, which I'd had packed away for days. I pulled on a black minidress with strappy sandals, knowing that heels would kill me in the field all night.

It was still hot so I didn't pile on the makeup and just used a little mascara. It was easier to hide behind a gallon of eyeliner and shadow, but I knew E could see through it all anyway.

Before pulling on a black T-shirt that matched his jeans, Derek eyed me up and down. "You look hot."

"Thanks." I ran my fingers through my hair as I watched him put on his leather wrist cuffs. "You want me to let everyone know we're ready?"

He nodded as he searched for his black boots.

I tried not to look too eager as I hurried from the room and made my way to E's door. I knocked quickly as I stared down the hall to make sure Derek hadn't come out.

As soon as E answered, his arm looped around my waist and pulled me in and against his body as I melted into him.

"We can't do this," I panted as my eyes fell closed. It was too painful to look at his perfect face and tell him no.

"Friends hug," he whispered into my ear, and I shivered. But by now, we were in too deep. We both knew it was more.

He pulled back to look me in the eye before he pressed his lips to my forehead and nodded. We slipped into the hall and I sighed with relief that no one had come out of his or her room yet.

I went to Donna's door and E went to the twins'. We smiled stupidly at each other as we waited for them to answer. Derek came out and snuck up behind me, pressing himself against my back. E's face went hard and he turned to look ahead. Thankfully, the twins answered and he went inside their room. Donna called out that she was coming, and a few seconds later her door popped open as she fastened an earring in her ear.

"You look great." She smiled at me approvingly.

"Thanks. You, too," I said, looking over her jean skirt and off-the-shoulder black blouse.

"Can we talk?"

"About?" I had the sudden urge to flee the room. The last

person I wanted to have a talk with was the girlfriend of the guy I was secretly falling for.

"I know you and E are close, and I am probably the last person you want bringing this up to you, but it is no secret that he cares about you."

"We are just friends." Saying that out loud was physically painful, but I wasn't about to lay all of my secrets on the table for E's girlfriend.

She studied me for a minute and sighed loudly. "He's a good guy that I care about a lot. I don't want to see him hurt."

That was the last thing I wanted as well. The thought of hurting E or Derek killed me inside, and I knew it was inevitable. If now Donna was bringing it up, I knew I would soon have to decide what I was going to do.

She held my gaze for another moment before glancing away as the guys approached. "Tuck just called. He got us a limo for the event. Tickets are waiting at the gate." She slipped on one of her sandals, trying to balance on one foot.

E slipped in beside us and I didn't miss the brush of his fingers along my hip. He stood next to Donna, letting her hold his arm while she slid on her other shoe.

"This should be fun," I said, trying to sound cheery.

I WASN'T A fan of long car rides, but if I had to choose, I would ride in a limo everywhere I go. We toasted to friendship, to music, and to every other excuse we could find to have another drink. Forty-five minutes in, the music was blaring and the guys were drunkenly singing along.

I forced myself not to stare at E when his voice reminded me of his singing with me last night.

I closed my eyes and blocked out all of the other voices so I could focus only on him.

"You all right?" Derek bumped his shoulder against mine, and the pain from my bruise caused my eyes to shoot open.

E leaned forward as if he wanted to say or do something to comfort me, but his body froze as Derek's arm went around me.

"What's wrong?" Derek pressed his forehead against mine and I shrugged, hating myself for making E watch this.

"We're here," Chris yelled, and everyone cheered. Everyone except E and me. His eyes just focused on the glass in his hand.

We filed out of the car and made our way to the ticket office set up on the corner of the field where we needed to pick up our tickets. The ground was soft from recent rain, and I frowned as I thought about ruining my shoes. I glanced up at the sky, which was covered in feathery, white clouds, but it didn't look as if rain was a threat today. The place was chaos as fans swarmed the gates and heavy rock music played in the distance. Women wore next to nothing or were drowning in tie-dye T-shirts. The crowd was incredibly diverse given that some of the bands were older and from a time when rock had a political message, and other bands were just starting out and their focus had more of a darker tone.

The smell of fried food intermingled with pot filled the air, and I briefly wondered if the promoters looked the other way at people's smoking marijuana, just to sell more food. Groupies clung to anyone who was covered in tats, and a few feet away someone was strumming a guitar as a group of people, sitting in a circle around him, sang along. It reminded me of when I went to vacation Bible school when I was nine and we all sang hymns as the pastor played the guitar. Even then, I enjoyed it so much I wanted to go to church every day just so I could sing. Funny how life changes in the blink of an eye.

I got lost in thought as I watched a woman spinning slowly, her arms out to her sides and face to the sky. She was smiling as she danced in her bare feet to a rhythm of her own. The crowd grew louder to my left, pulling me from my thoughts. An old school bus hand-painted with messages of peace and love had just emptied out, and its passengers were making their way toward the gates. They smelled like stale beer and sweat. Luckily, we were escorted through a private entrance after Donna spoke to someone in charge.

The swarm of people was unbelievable, and we had to fight our way to get anywhere, but the crowd was mostly peaceful because the sun had yet to set. As they say, the freaks come out at night. This was especially true in the rock-and-roll world. Something about the music just made people go wild. Trash already littered the ground, and in typical rock-and-roll fashion, a few arguments had already broken out, and several women were already in various stages of undress as onlookers shot pictures with their cell phones. I shook my head as we walked around them. I could never live without music, but the partying that went hand in hand with it wasn't really my scene.

Long Neck was onstage singing a soulful ballad from the seventies titled "Missing My Misses," so we weren't in any danger of getting hurt from a mosh pit. Although I had no doubt that it would all change after the sun set.

"You all right?" I asked E as we followed behind Tucker. He nodded but did not look at me, and my heart sank a little, unable to keep up with his whiplash emotions.

We stopped walking as we reached the middle of the crowd. I slid up beside Cass and began to dance, getting lost in the music, my favorite escape. I didn't want to think about Derek or E. My heart was being ripped in two, and I couldn't be that girl. I had committed myself to Derek and I wasn't going to screw that up. I needed to solve the problems within me first. I needed to figure out how to keep myself looking forward and not focused on the pain that sometimes threatened to consume me.

I always thought Derek was perfect because he accepted that I struggled with physical intimacy and he didn't ask me about my sadness, but now that someone cared enough to know the truth, I wanted to tell the truth and finally set myself free from the cage I kept myself in.

AS NIGHT FELL the drinks continued to flow freely and the crowd became more amped with each set. I tried to focus my attention on Derek as Donna whispered into E's ear and he laughed at whatever she had said. It was like a punch in the gut to see them being openly affectionate in public. I hated myself for wishing it were me who was making him laugh right now. Derek turned my necklace so the clasp was at the back of my neck. My fingers automatically went to the small star pendant that he had gotten for me. His lips were at my ear as his arms went around my waist and he pulled my back against him.

"My favorite rock star," he whispered as his lips pressed against the side of my neck. I slid my hand back into his long hair, holding his lips to me. "Have you thought any more about going to Texas with me when this is over?"

I shrugged as I watched E, his back to me and Donna at his side, her hand on his back.

Derek turned me to face him, his eyes searching mine as he tucked my hair behind my ear. "I think it would be good for you to meet my family. Maybe we could . . . take the next step in our relationship."

My mouth dropped open. Was he talking about getting engaged? Did he finally want to give me the commitment I so desperately craved from him? I felt sick, confused. Part of me wondered why he suddenly wanted to bring me into his family. Why was all of this happening now? Now that I was the one questioning my feelings? Derek was suddenly giving me what I had always thought I wanted, and E had made it very clear in the past that he didn't want a family, or at least didn't deserve one. So . . . what was I doing? How long could this go on? I would only be around E for another week and a half during this vacation, and then my life would go back to normal, or as normal as can be expected for someone in a band. Was I willing to throw it all away for a few days of fun? I realized he was still staring at me and waiting for my reaction.

"I'd like that." I couldn't muster much more. My voice cracked, but Derek didn't seem to notice as he pulled me into his arms and hugged me.

CHAPTER

Twenty-Five

ERIC

I CHANCED A GLANCE over my shoulder at Sarah, who was wrapped in Derek's arms; his eyes narrowed at me and I nodded, taking a drink from my beer.

He wasn't going to go away easy. He didn't care about what was best for her. He was a selfish prick, and all my presence had done was make him cling harder to her to prove that he could beat me, as if this were some fucking game or some shit. I put my arm around Donna's neck as I looked ahead at the stage, wondering when I would get another moment alone with Sarah.

This wasn't all in my head, right? No. It couldn't be.

"You all right?" Donna looked up at me, her eyebrows pulled together with concern.

I smiled, not wanting to worry her any more with my shit. "I'm fine. Just wondering when the good bands are going to play," I joked. She rolled her eyes and laid her head against my shoulder. I couldn't stop the nagging feeling from the back of my mind that when all of this was said and done, I would be left completely alone.

It felt inevitable. Like watching a coming train wreck but being unable to stop it. Who was I to stand up against the train, or the overwhelming desire to be with Sarah?

"I'm going to get another drink. You want something?" I asked Donna, trying to mask the pain in my voice. She shook her head no and took a step away from me. I made my way into the crowd, disappearing into the sea of bodies, wanting to just get lost in the people, the music and in life. Cryptic was onstage and the crowd was becoming more crazy by the second. The band's music seemed as if it could induce seizures, and I was glad we'd found a spot near the stage so we wouldn't be in the middle of the frenzy if the crowd got too out of hand. The angry music was doing nothing to help my mood. I didn't want to slip back into the old me who used violence when shit didn't go my way.

I bought myself a drink and poured it down my throat, hoping to push back some of the sadness that was creeping over me.

I contemplated walking up to Sarah and taking her in my arms, and I would have if I knew that was what she wanted. If only I could get her alone again. I needed to tell her how I felt.

But instead I wandered off, walking along the tents that lined the back of the field and looking over all of the merchandise for sale. I didn't want to mask my feelings with a smile. I wanted to be alone with who I really was. Sarah was with someone else, Donna wanted more than I could ever give her. I could hear the train whistle blowing in the distance, and instead of stepping back to watch, I wanted to stand on the tracks. I didn't want to be left standing if it meant standing alone.

"You don't look so good," Terry called from my left.

"Thanks." I shook my head as my eyes danced over leather belts and buckles.

"You don't ever make life easy, do ya?"

"It's not in my nature." I laughed sardonically and took another drink.

"I know you probably don't care if this ends up hurting you in the end, but have you thought about what it will do to Sarah?"

My eyes met his. "Every fucking second."

"And Donna?" He cocked an eyebrow.

"Donna is just looking for some company."

"Oh? She could have found it in my brother. You know that fucker isn't picky."

"Still bitter about Lizzy?"

Terry shook his head and looked off at the leather goods ahead of us. "Nah . . . he did me a favor with that one. Stop changing the fucking subject."

"What do you want me to say? Huh? The world is full of disappointment. Donna knew from day one that I was hung up on Sarah."

"She wants you, dumbass. And you aren't exactly sending her clear signals."

"Spare me the fucking lecture. Sarah is with Derek. She is never going to leave him. Am I supposed to just never be with anyone?"

"You're thinking with the wrong head, man."

"Nah . . . I'm thinking with my heart. Even worse."

Terry patted me on the shoulder as he sighed loudly. "Fuck, man. Promise me you'll keep your cool." His eyes met mine and I could already feel my blood begin to boil. "Derek is telling everyone he is taking her to Texas to meet his family."

"What?" I didn't mean to yell but I was completely blindsided. "No." I shook my head. "She wouldn't do that."

"She didn't deny it, man. She was right there." I glared over at him and he ran his hand over his hair. "I'm gonna give you a minute to think over what you want to do about that. Just . . . if she seems happy, isn't that what you want?"

I nodded but I was crushed. I knew she was feeling what I was, and deep down she knew what kind of person Derek was. I threw my can in the trash and ordered another drink. I preferred to forget this trip altogether. It would all be over in two weeks anyway. Maybe Terry was right and I just needed to fucking get over it and move on. Somehow.

CHAPTER

Twenty-Six

SARAH

As the sun began to sink, the bands got better. The only thing missing was E, who had disappeared about an hour ago. I tried to focus on the lyrics as the singer belted her heart out onstage, but I couldn't get E out of my mind.

A friend could worry about a friend. That's what I told myself as I scanned the crowd for him. Derek's arms tightened around my waist as he danced behind me, but I just swayed my hips slightly, not feeling up to dancing.

The idea of leaving California after our vacation and heading straight to Texas freaked me out. Derek grew up with his grandmother and his older brother, who was off in Texas working as a lawyer. How much trouble could one little old lady be? But I still couldn't settle my stomach at the thought of meeting anyone's family. I knew what kind of secrets can be hidden behind locked doors.

"You all right?" Cass asked, pulling me from my thoughts.

"Yeah." I shrugged.

"I'm going to grab Tuck a drink. You want to come?"

"Sure," I replied with a little too much enthusiasm. Derek released his hold on me and Cass and I wove our way through the crowd to the tents set up in the back.

"You doing okay? You looked a little out of it back there."

"I'm nervous about meeting Derek's family." I shrugged.

"Yeah, I get that. Meeting Dorris was a real . . . fun experience." Cass laughed.

"You're not helping." I laughed and a hand landed on my hip.

"Maybe I can help," E whispered into my ear, and Cass grinned as my face flushed.

"I'm gonna grab the drinks." Cass turned and made her way to the tent, leaving me alone with E. I turned around to face him.

He smiled as he ran the pad of his thumb over my cheek. "I went off for a drink and you moved on with your life." He put his hand over his heart dramatically and swayed slightly.

"How many of those drinks have you had? You've been gone a long time."

"Long enough for you to make plans to meet Derek's family?" E cocked his head, and even though his tone was playful, I knew his mood was anything but.

"We're friends, E." It hurt to look him in the eye and lie about what I was feeling in my heart.

"Yeah?" He reached out and took my hand, his fingertips rubbing over my knuckles. "You don't feel that?" He leaned in closer and his lips brushed against my earlobe. I shivered at the touch. "You don't feel this, Sarah?"

I closed my eyes as I forced my body not to melt against his and shook my head. It was painful and he pulled back, nodding.

"I must have imagined it then. I apologize." The muscles in his jaw jumped under the skin as his eyes searched mine for the truth, and of course he could see it. E could always see right through me like no one else.

"E . . ." I wanted to say so many things, but the words didn't seem as if they would do the situation justice. I had fucked up beyond belief, and making it right would mean hurting the one person who seemed to get me, but E was a wild card. Derek had promised commitment and I needed that. I craved it.

"It's fine, Sarah. I just want you to be happy. That's all I ever wanted."

"I know that."

He pulled me in for a hug, and as much as I wanted to resist, my body wouldn't let me. My hands slid over the tight muscles of his back as his hands trailed up and down my spine. He pressed his lips against my throat and I sighed.

His body stiffened momentarily. "You can't make little

noises like that when I have you in my arms." He groaned as he held me tighter. I tried to pull back but he wasn't letting me budge.

"E, I'm sorry."

"Shh . . . don't say you're sorry. Sorry means you regret it and I know you don't."

"I will *never* regret you, E. You are my best friend and there are no words for how much I care about you."

"There's a word for how I feel about *you*." He pulled back to look me in the eye and my heart crumbled.

"I think we should probably head back." This time when I pulled away, he let his hands fall to his sides. The look on his face destroyed me. I could feel my world spiraling but I had no choice but to hold on and hope for the best. Derek had changed, and for me to hurt him now the way he had hurt me in the past would be a horrible betrayal. I couldn't help the way I was feeling, but I could stop myself from acting on those feelings.

"Are you ready?" Cass asked as her eyes darted between us.

I nodded as I sniffled, hating myself. Cass looked to E, who was still staring at me, his eyes burning through me.

"Yeah. We're done." He turned and walked into the crowd. Cass gave me a sympathetic look before we followed behind him.

I took a drink from her hand and took a big gulp, hoping it would settle my nerves. I knew the rest of the night was going to be excruciating.

CHAPTER
Twenty-Seven

ERIC

I COULDN'T CLEAR MY thoughts as I navigated us back to the rest of the band. I wanted to flip out and scream at Sarah for playing with my emotions, but I knew without a doubt she never meant to break my heart. I also knew that she was hurting every bit as much as I was. I could see the pain in her eyes. I just didn't know if the pain was from wanting to be with me or from not wanting to hurt me.

Either way, the damage was done. Sarah had made her choice and I wouldn't interfere with what she wanted.

I'd be a liar if I said I wasn't pissed, but most of that was directed at myself and Derek. I tried to plaster on a smile as I made my way to Donna.

"Where have you been?" She cocked an eyebrow at me.

"I got lost, but I found my way back to you."

"Aww . . . You're drunk," she joked as she wrapped her arms around my waist from the side. I draped and arm around her and kissed the top of her head.

"It improves my dance skills."

"I think you dance just fine." She glanced up at me and I shot her a wink. Although I wasn't exactly sober the day we practically fucked on the dance floor, there was no denying that we had chemistry.

"I had a good partner."

"Just good, huh?" She pressed her head against my chest, and even though I was dying inside, Donna always managed to make me laugh.

I was thankful that it was now dark and I wouldn't have to see Derek with his hands all over Sarah.

"Do you ever think you will get past what your ex did? Move on and get married?"

She shook her head as she stared off at the stage. "You?"

"Nah. Not the marrying type."

"I envy them." She nodded toward Tucker and Cass, and we both watched them for a moment as I ran my hand up and down Donna's back. What they had wasn't in the cards for me. Every time I put myself out there, I got hurt and I couldn't take much more.

"They make it not look so bad." Donna laughed sadly and I kissed her hair.

"You will have that. You're too good of a person not to."

"And what about you? You think you're a bad person?"

I glanced back up at the stage. A new band was getting ready to perform, and the crowd was getting louder. I never answered her and she didn't push me any further.

One band blended into the next, but anything was better than being locked up in that hotel room. I felt as if I were slowly losing my mind with every passing day.

"If you didn't get this gig, where do you think you would be?" I asked.

"I'd probably be backstage at this concert begging bands to let me work for them," she said with a laugh.

"This is your dream? You never wanted to do something else?"

She thought it over for a minute and shrugged. "I wanted to get married and have children."

"So you're just going to let one asshole kill your dreams?"

She glared up at me and back to the stage. "Dreams change, people change. I don't think I would be that good of a mother."

"Are you kidding? Look at how you take care of the band. You're a natural."

"I am kind of amazing."

I laughed as I squeezed her against my side.

"What about you? You want kids?"

"I'm not really a good role model for children. I can't even get my own shit together, I couldn't put a kid through that."

"You know, you're not half as bad as you think you are."

"Opinions may vary." I glanced over my shoulder to Sarah.

CHAPTER

Twenty-Eight

SARAH

*I*T HURT LIKE hell to look E in the eye and tell him that it was never going to happen with us. He deserved so much better than I could ever give him. I was a broken mess, too damaged for anyone to take on.

It was better this way.

I was thankful Derek never questioned my crazy mood swings or pushed me to open up more about my past, although it made me feel alone even when I was by his side. At times I wanted to speak up and explain why I was feeling the way I was, but I didn't know what I would do with myself if Derek didn't want me anymore and I was left by myself. After we went to Texas, things would only get better for us.

I squeezed Derek's hand as I watched his profile. He was

cheering for the band and I couldn't help but smile at how excited he got over music. It had always been an escape for me.

"They're good," I shouted over the crowd.

Derek's eyes met mine. "We're better." He smirked as he pulled my hand to his mouth and kissed it. I smiled up at him, and he turned to face me. He breathed deeply, as if about to say something important. "Okay, now, don't get mad."

My first reaction was to narrow my eyes and prepare for him to break my heart, but what he said next nearly knocked me off my feet.

"I bought tickets the other day. To Texas. We leave the day after tomorrow."

I stood frozen. I was relieved that he was serious about us, but then the anger started to set in. "How did you know I was going to say yes?"

"Why wouldn't you?" His eyes narrowed.

I felt like an asshole. "I mean, leaving early. You know how much I've missed Cass. This may be the last chance to spend time with her for months."

He sighed as if he had expected me to say something else. "We need to focus on us now." His hand slid over the side of my neck as he leaned in closer. "I love you, Sarah. I thought you loved me, too."

"I do love you, but . . ."

"But nothing. Either you want to be with me or you can

fucking leave," he snapped, and I pulled back from him, shocked by his sudden change in attitude. "I'm sorry. I didn't mean it like that." He ran his hands roughly through his long, dark hair.

"I'm not leaving." I could feel the tears forming in my eyes.

"Good." He stepped toward me again with a smirk on his face, but I took a step back to keep distance between us.

"No. I mean I am not leaving my friend early." I crossed my arms over my chest.

"Fine." His face was nearly touching mine and anger radiated off him. "Then *I* am leaving." Derek took off through the crowd and I called after him, but he never stopped and my pleas were drowned out by the music.

I hung my head, not sure how everything went from cloud nine to a disaster so quickly. I wanted to chase after him and tell him I was sorry, but I couldn't move.

"You okay?" Cass asked, placing her hand on my back. I didn't turn to look at her. I didn't want to ruin this time for everyone else. I nodded and tried my best to put a smile on my face. "It looked like you were fighting."

"We're fine." I tried to sound cheery, but I knew my voice gave me away. "He just . . . wasn't feeling well."

"Did he leave without you?"

"Well . . . it's not like I'm alone or anything." I tried to play it off as if it were no big deal, but she wrapped her arms around me and pulled me in for a hug, and I couldn't stop a tear from falling on her shoulder.

"Come on." She pulled me toward Tucker, and I realized that everyone was watching me and I froze, pulling out of her grasp.

"Actually, I think I need a drink."

She looked at me, unsure, but nodded and let her hand fall. I wanted to run, run to Derek, run from him.

As I turned to walk away, I heard a girl scream Tucker's name. Cass grabbed my arm to keep us from getting separated as the people around us began to chant his name over and over, growing louder and louder. *Tuck-er! Tuck-er!*

"This could get really ugly if we don't get out of this crowd," she said wearily as E's arm came around my waist. It didn't matter what was going on, he always put me first.

"You guys wanna play?" Tuck's eyes moved between us, and I glanced up at E.

"If Sarah plays."

A knowing smile spread across Tuck's lips, and he nodded once and turned to pull Cass from the crowd. E and I followed with the twins at our sides.

As we reached security at the side of the stage, they stopped us. "You have to have a pass to get back here," the man said with his hand up in front of Tucker's chest.

"Tuck?" a voice called from behind the man, and Danny

Demon, the lead singer of Crash and Burn, came over to embrace Tucker in a hug. I grew up listening to their music and it was surreal to see him standing before us in the flesh. If I wanted to, I could reach out and touch his green Mohawk . . . I had to hold back from doing so.

"You doing next year's Music Awards? That was dope. Heard about the proposal. Congrats, man," Danny said with a slight Irish accent.

"It's been a minute, man. How you been?"

"Just livin', man. Tiny, let them back. They're my friends and the crowd is about to rip them apart."

The security guard sighed and rolled his eyes but stepped out of the way for us to get behind the stage. Once we were out of the crowd I began to relax in E's arm, but he did not let me go.

"Who's up next?" Tuck asked as Danny walked ahead of us.

"We're up in ten. You guys looking to perform?"

Tucker nodded, and Danny grinned from ear to ear. E dropped his hold on my waist and spoke directly into Tucker's ear.

"Not exactly how you pictured your honeymoon, huh?" I gave Cass a half smile.

"It's fine. Nothing really compares to seeing Tucker up on-stage, and as long as we're not on that stupid tour bus, I can deal with it."

Tucker's arm went over Cass's shoulders, and he pressed a kiss to her temple and then asked me, "You good with a duet for 'Loved'?"

I nodded but my nerves were on edge. I had never performed without Derek, and he was nowhere to be found.

We stood by the stairs to the stage as Danny Demon introduced us, and the reaction of the crowd caught me off guard. It was hard to see outside the bubble we were in while touring and spending all of our time on buses. The crowd was deafening, and it was the first time I realized how big Damaged had grown. It was a high unlike anything else I had ever experienced.

As the opening notes to the song began to play, the crowd quieted and my nerves dissipated. The music pulsed through the speakers around us and I could feel it vibrating through my body. It became its own living creature and we were wrapped inside it. The stage was my home. It was where I felt safe and one of the only places I could always count on to let my walls down.

I closed my eyes as I sang along, wishing I never had to leave the stage.

In a crowded room, you're all I see.
So thought consumed, baby let it be . . .
The past can haunt, but it cannot touch.
You've given your all and loved too much.

Take my hand, let me lead . . .
You're loved too, baby, and you belong with me . . .

None of my problems mattered, none of my secrets were hidden. I could let everything out and people wouldn't judge me. I had heard Tucker sing this song a thousand times, but never truly understood how much pain went into it until the words came from my own lips. It was about watching someone you loved being hurt by someone else and vowing to be there when everything crashed down for the person. I knew why it meant so much for Tuck, and now it meant something for me.

As the song came to an end, I smiled out at the never-ending sea of people before turning to follow the twins offstage, on cloud nine from my music therapy, but a hand grabbed my arm to stop me. I turned to look up at E, and my heart beat out of my chest and everyone faded to black around us.

"We have to sing our song," he said with a grin. I halfheartedly pulled against his grip as I shook my head, unable to keep the smile from my face. In this moment, I knew two things. It was wrong for me to sing a song about my feelings for E when I knew Derek was out in that crowd somewhere, and there was no way I could say no as E looked at me expectantly. I nodded once and E pulled me into his arms for a quick hug. He grabbed a guitar from Danny and perched himself on the edge of a stool. I stood by his side with a mic in hand as my heart raced.

E began to strum the guitar as he looked up to me. His voice was low and haunting as he began to sing.

> *The flames lick at my fingertips as I'm drawn to the fire,*
> *I want to run but I'm consumed by the overwhelming*
>   *desire . . .*

I joined him, singing the next several lines, his eyes never leaving mine. I wanted this song to last forever, and that is when I remembered we had never written the ending. But E looked calm and completely at ease as we sang through the chorus. He continued the song after what we had written together, and I could only stand there in front of thousands of people while he told me everything he was feeling.

> *My heart skips from your glance and I can't look away,*
> *You'll break me but take me, there's no other way,*
> *Life on the road, babe, I'm a rolling stone,*
> *No matter where life takes us, you'll always be my home.*

We sang through the chorus one last time, and it took everything inside me to keep my voice from shaking. The crowd erupted in applause, but all I could hear was the thudding of my heart in my ears. E stood, guitar in hand, and pulled me into his arms. I felt safe and I knew he would always be home for me, too. I glanced out over the people below the stage, and my eyes locked on Derek's. His expression was a mixture of anger and pain, and it physically hurt me to see that look. It was the same look that had echoed on my face when he had cheated on me so long ago. I pulled back from E, not able to look to him and see the hurt in his eyes. This was what Cass had warned me about. This was what I had been trying to avoid. I could barely breathe around the lump that had formed in my throat as I ran off the stage, leaving E standing alone. I screamed Derek's name while shoving through the fans to get to him so I could explain, but he was gone.

THE NIGHT WAS slowly winding down and I hated that I would soon have to go back to the hotel and find out if I had been abandoned by Derek or if he would be waiting for me. I wasn't sure which I preferred, and I felt horrible for even feeling that way.

I didn't know what I would do if he was gone. Without the band I had no one. My mother was only a few hours away, but that was never an option. I hadn't spoken to her in years.

I tried to keep a smile on my face, but I was cracking. I needed to see Derek so I could find out where we stood. I felt as if I were being taken to my execution as we made our way to the limo. The twins talked animatedly about all the women they had hit on at the concert, Cass and Tucker were whispering to each other, and Donna was debating bands with E. I was completely alone, surrounded by my friends. I stared off toward the heavily tinted windows, but it was nighttime and I couldn't see anything besides an occasional streetlight. I ran my hand over the black leather seat beside me, tracing the stitching with my fingertip. Derek should have been at my side.

"You okay?" E's voice cut through my thoughts, and I glanced up at him. He was sitting low in his seat, his hands behind his head, eyes locked on me. Donna was busy playing with her phone and didn't seem to care that he was watching me. I knew my running off the stage had hurt him, but I wasn't ready to deal with that now. I couldn't handle much more of any of this.

"I'm fine." I smiled, mask in place. I looked back toward the window knowing damn well E could see through my lies. Maybe I should have told Derek I would leave for Texas early with him. What was stopping me? He was finally making the commitment and I was telling him to wait.

We pulled up outside the hotel and I was becoming increasingly nervous. I had no idea what I would do if he wasn't inside.

No one spoke as we rode the elevator to our floor. Everyone parted ways as we hit the third floor, but I lingered behind, not wanting anyone to see if Derek had left. I watched as everyone paired off, except for E and Donna. He walked her to her door and told her good-night before walking past me to his room. He paused outside his door, staring at me. I slid in my card and pushed the door open and walked inside.

It was empty and I wanted to scream, but I saw Derek's bag still on the floor. He hadn't left the state, but he sure as hell hadn't come back here. I pulled out my phone and dialed his number. It rang and rang until his voice mail picked up. I hung up and tossed my phone on the bed. I jumped at the sound of a soft knock on the open door behind me and spun around.

"You still okay?" E asked, his head cocked to the side.

"Yeah." I smiled, trying to hide my sadness. "He didn't leave. His bags are here."

"But he's not?"

"No." I looked over at his bag on the floor.

"Yeah, I didn't think he would be."

"He's not that guy anymore." I hated defending him, especially to E.

My phone rang and I jumped again, grabbing it off the bed. "It's Derek."

E just nodded and pulled the door to my room closed as I answered. I was relieved he had left me alone because I had no idea how Derek was going to act. I squeezed my eyes shut.

"Hey." I tried to sound cheery.

"You alone?" Derek's words were slurred and it sounded as if he was in a bar or a club.

"Of course. I just got back. I'm glad you didn't leave."

"Why would I leave? I paid for the room." His voice was cold and it felt as if I had been punched in the stomach, but I deserved it.

"I'm sorry . . . about earlier. I do want to meet your family."

"Yeah? I'm leaving day after tomorrow. I want you with me."

"I will be."

"I love you so much, Sarah."

"I love you, too."

He hung up the phone and I leaned against the wall as I thought about having to leave all of my friends. I knew I wouldn't get to see them again for a long time, and it killed me.

CHAPTER

Twenty-Nine

ERIC

LAY IN MY bed recounting the night. It made me ill to think of anyone ever hurting Sarah, and I knew in time Derek would break her heart again. She was already so fragile there was no telling what it would do to her. When I saw him below the stage, I knew things were only going to get worse for her.

The phone rang next to my bed and I ignored it, but whoever it was called back immediately. I reluctantly pulled myself from my thoughts and picked up the receiver.

"Hey," Sarah said with a loud sigh.

"You okay?"

She laughed and I could picture her shaking her head. "I'm fine. You don't always need to ask me that."

"I just don't want you to be upset."

"I'm going to Texas, E," she blurted out. I ran my hand over my jaw as I let that sink in once again.

"When?"

"Day after tomorrow. It's for the best."

"For who?" I couldn't hide my anger.

"We've already been through this."

"But things have changed."

"Nothing's changed, E. I shouldn't have told him I wouldn't go."

"Is he there?"

"No. He probably won't be for a while. I think he was partying."

I hung up and made my way to her room. I was only wearing my jeans and I didn't bother to put on a shirt. I needed to say a proper good-bye. Once Derek was back, I knew he wouldn't let me have a moment alone with her and he was right not to.

I knocked on her door, running my hand over my hair as I waited for her to answer. She pulled the door open slowly, her sad eyes meeting mine.

"You can't leave."

"E," she sighed, and shook her head slowly, her hair falling around her face.

I stepped around her, slamming the door behind me and then pacing the floor of her room. "He is no good for you, Sarah."

She followed me toward the bed, sitting down on the edge as I continued to walk the length of the room.

"I can't just sit back and watch him hurt you anymore."

"*This* hurts, E."

I stopped and turned to look at her, saw the pain in her eyes. "Do you have any idea how much you mean to me?" I was trying to keep calm, but it was virtually impossible. She hung her head as her nails dug into her knees leaving tiny, red half-moon indents.

"You can't do this. Don't do to Donna what he's done to me."

I leaned down over Sarah, my hands on either side of her, pressing into the mattress. "I am *nothing* like him."

"I know that." Her voice was small. "I won't be like him either. I'm taken, E. As long as he is faithful to me, I won't go behind his back."

"Faithful? You think just because I haven't *fucked* you that you haven't already cheated on Derek?"

Her hand cracked across my face and her nostrils flared in anger as she narrowed her eyes.

I stood up, running my hand over my cheek. "I shouldn't have said that . . ."

She held up her hand to stop me from talking as she pushed from the bed. She walked around me and opened the door to the room, her head hung as she waited for me to leave.

"I will miss you . . . so much," she said quietly.

I nodded, walking toward her, stopping just inches from her. She refused to look me in the eye. "I won't try again, Sarah. If I walk out now, I'm done."

A small sob ripped from her chest but she nodded slowly. It was physically painful to walk out of Sarah's life, but I knew from the beginning this was the way it would end.

I made my way back to my room and picked up Sarah's guitar,

which still sat propped against the wall. I began to strum the notes to our song. It was fitting that we never finished it together, just as we would never finish what had begun between us. Every word I sang to her I meant.

As I continued to play, I thought of all the ways my life had gone wrong. Every path I chose when I knew it would only hurt me, every person I tried to love when I knew I would never get it in return. I played for hours until my fingertips were numb and I knew what I needed to do.

There was a woman who wanted my company, who desperately craved someone to love her, and maybe I could be that man for her.

Donna was amazing. She was kind and funny and didn't look at me as if I were a mistake. I could be whom she wanted and I knew it would never be thrown back in my face.

It didn't take long for me to make my way to her room. She had been sleeping and pushed her hair back from her face. Even when woken in the middle of the night, she was absolutely stunning.

I had a hand braced on either side of the doorframe. She smiled when she saw me and I couldn't help but smile back at her. I reached out, running my hand over the soft angles of her jaw. She stepped forward and pressed her lips against mine. I groaned as my hand slid back into her hair, and I ran my tongue over her lower lip. Her body pressed into mine and I moaned at the physical contact I craved. I needed to feel wanted just as much as she did, and we moved against each other with an incredible hunger.

I needed to move on and make myself forget, and Donna needed the same from me. I saw it now. She wasn't asking anything from me that I couldn't give her. She just didn't want to be alone. Together we could help heal old wounds and learn to move forward. I stepped forward and pushed the door closed behind me. I slipped her night-gown off her shoulders and reluctantly pulled my mouth from hers as I tugged it down over her breasts and it pooled at her feet. She was incredibly beautiful and I was a fool for not seeing it sooner. My hand slid roughly over her breast as I walked us toward her bed, not able to wait any longer to mask the ache in my chest.

CHAPTER Thirty

SARAH

I AWOKE TO DEREK'S climbing into bed just after three in the morning. His hand slid over my breast roughly as he pushed his lips hard against mine. I shoved against his chest, but he pinned my shoulder down with his.

"Get off me!" I could smell the alcohol coming off him in waves and it was nauseating.

He reluctantly rolled off me. "Fuck," he barked loudly as his fists came down against the bed. "What is wrong with you?"

I got up from the bed and went to the kitchen area, filling a small glass with water and drinking it down quickly as I struggled to slow my breathing.

"You caught me off guard." I refilled my cup and drank more slowly this time.

"You were expecting someone else?" he said angrily.

I rolled my eyes. "No, Derek. I only have you." It was painful even to say the words but it was the truth now. I had pushed away the one person who gave a damn about me for Derek, and now he was throwing it in my face. Now instead of feeling empty I felt heartbroken.

I set my cup in the sink and made my way to the desk, turning on the small table lamp so I could write. He immediately jumped from the bed to follow me.

"I have fucking needs, Sarah." He stood over me from behind.

"I'm just not in the mood."

"That's the fucking point! You're never in the mood anymore. Ever since we came here."

"You know that's not true, Derek." I sighed as a tear fell to my paper, and I hunched over farther so he couldn't see it.

"Yeah, well, it's getting fucking old. Maybe I should find someone who actually wants me."

"Maybe you should." I rolled my eyes and tried to focus on the paper.

"Fine." He stomped across the room and I jumped as the hotel-room door slammed hard. I scrambled to my feet and grabbed the tiny trash can in the kitchen as I heaved the contents of my stomach into it.

I slid down on the cool tile floor, my back against the counter as the room began to spin. I was losing control. I tried to push out the fear and sadness, welcoming the familiar emptiness that had kept me together for all of these years. I needed to shut it all off, but the hurt hung thick in the air around me. It was all I could see, feel, and breathe. I was consumed by the pain and there was no escaping it.

I wrapped my arms around my knees, hugging myself as I rocked slowly and sang in my head, begging reality to shut off.

It felt like hours, days even, that I tried to calm myself, praying that Derek would come back and tell me it was all going to be okay. But I knew that wouldn't happen. That wasn't who he was. I knew exactly what he was doing.

I thought of my father's old, rusty razor, caked in dried blood. I wanted the release, a place for the feelings to go. I wanted the tangible proof of the pain that was consuming me from the inside out. Maybe if Derek saw it, he wouldn't be able to deny what he was doing to me. Maybe then he would stop and things could change.

I pulled myself up on shaky legs as I glanced around the room with blurred vision. Stumbling into the bedroom, I grabbed my iPod and hooked it into my portable speakers, finding my favorite escape easily. The sound of Lynyrd Skynyrd filled the room as I let the sobs rip from my chest.

I struggled against the overwhelming urge, squeezing my fists so tightly, my nails dig into the tender flesh of my palms. The small bite of pain was not enough of a release. I stalked off to the bathroom and pulled open the shower curtain. My razor sat on the edge of the tub, begging me to use it. I was like a druggie needing a fix. The urge was overwhelming. It was no longer a matter of if but when.

I cupped my hand over my mouth as the hurt overwhelmed me. Only one thing could take that away, make me feel better.

I spun around and pulled open the door to my room and made my way to E.

CHAPTER

Thirty-One

ERIC

THE SUN WAS about to come up as I returned to my room, but I couldn't sleep.

When a knock came at the door, I laughed to myself as I made my way to pull it open, expecting to see Donna, though I had just left her room ten minutes before. My heart stopped as I locked eyes with Sarah. Her face was pink and damp from crying.

"What did he do?" I glanced down the hall but all was quiet, and I looked back to her in confusion as she wrung her hands together nervously.

"Nothing. Can I come in?" Her chest jumped as she struggled to calm her breathing. I nodded and took a step back as she slipped inside, and I closed the door behind her. I ran my hand through my hair as the smell of her shampoo assaulted my senses. She walked over toward the bed, but had second thoughts about sitting on it.

I crossed the room and stood in front of her, forcing myself not to touch her. "Please, tell me why you're crying."

Her gaze fell to the floor between us and she wiped the back of her hand over her cheek and laughed nervously. "I'm a mess."

"You're beautiful." I don't know why I said it, but as her eyes met mine, I knew it was a mistake.

"Why can't he talk to me like that?"

I blew out a hard breath as I struggled not to let this massive kick to my ego upset me. I knew she was hurting. She didn't deserve what he put her through, even if she didn't leave him. For whatever reason, she felt she needed to stay. I think at first it had a lot to do with not wanting to be alone, but now it seemed more like guilt, and that blame rested entirely on me.

"Because he's a fucking idiot and he doesn't deserve you."

"I don't deserve *you*. I'm sorry for . . . everything."

"Don't be sorry. I only regret that it hurts you. I knew . . ." I cleared my throat, trying to force out the truth. "I knew I would never have you."

"I made a mistake." Her voice was small and she sounded so fragile. I could only nod. She was right. I was a mistake and for the rest of my life I would have to carry around with me the guilt of hurting her. "I should have chosen you."

I didn't think my heart could break any further, the pieces so small, but I was wrong and the pain ripped through my chest. "Don't say that. Not now. I can't take any more. There's been so much back-and-forth . . . I can't take it."

She took a step toward me and put her hand on my chest. Her touch was almost painful and I winced as the warmth of her fingertips slid over my skin.

"Now that I'm with someone else, now you want me?" I threw her own words back at her, and she flinched at my tone as if I had hit her.

"It's not like that, E. I've always . . . cared about you."

"But it won't ever be enough. You'd rather get walked over by that asshole until he breaks you so badly that you slip back into who you were." My gaze fell to the scars on her arms. I understood now. I wore the same scars on my heart. I would heal, but I would never be whole again.

"Please don't yell at me." Her voice was barely a whisper and I knew she was on the verge of tears again.

I wrapped my arms around her neck and held her against me. It was physically painful to stay away from her and equally so to hold her in my arms and know she would never be mine. "I'm so sorry, Sarah. So sorry for all of this. I should have never let you know what I was feeling."

"I'm glad you told me."

My grip tightened around her as tears filled my own eyes. "It just made everything worse for you. It was selfish of me."

"It's not selfish to tell someone that you care about them."

I pulled back from her so I could look her in the eye. "It was. I was putting my feelings before yours. I knew you and I would never hap-pen." I put my hands on the sides of her face, wanting desperately to pull her closer so I could kiss her. "I knew you could never care about me like I care about you." For the first time since I could remember, a tear slid down my cheek, but I didn't bother to wipe it away.

"I do care about you . . . so much." Her hands reached for my face but I grabbed them, holding them in mine as I closed my eyes, begging myself for strength.

"Please don't make me say no to you. I can't. I'm not strong enough." I shook my head as another tear fell. "I can't take much more of this. It's killing me. *You* are killing me, Sarah."

Sarah took a small step back, nodding as her own cheeks glistened with tears. She swallowed hard and pulled her fingers from mine. I ached to reach out and grab her again, but I forced myself to let her walk out of my life. It was for the best. I wouldn't be the other guy and I wouldn't do to Donna what her fiancé had. The door slammed to my room and to my heart.

I collapsed to my knees as I let the emotions rip through me. A knife to the chest would have been less painful, and at least eventually the torture would have ended.

CHAPTER

Thirty-Two

SARAH

I MADE MY WAY back to my room in a daze. The walls went up as I went into self-preservation mode. As I walked into the bedroom, my song blared on repeat through the tiny speakers on the desk. My eyes danced over the cramped space. I sank down into the chair at the desk and began to scribble down all of my pain, hoping the faster I wrote, the more I would bleed out on the paper and the less I'd have to really hurt myself.

> I can be anyone but never myself, locked away like a china doll,
>   kept prisoner on the shelf,

The words were too real, too painful even to write on paper. My mask had slipped and I could no longer keep the feelings at bay. I needed to let them come out or I would drown in my own sadness. I crawled into the center of the bed and pulled my knees to my chest as I let all of the memories and pain flood through me at once. My mother's indifference to my sadness, Phil's coldhearted remarks, his violating touch. I missed my father terribly and only wanted to have someone to share my feelings with. Jenny had been too young and didn't understand why I was always so depressed. I didn't understand myself why I couldn't just be happy. Not until I found music was I able to release all of the hurt that I kept inside.

Exhaustion took over and I cried myself to sleep. I wasn't sure if hours or just minutes had passed, but I awoke to the sound of the door opening. At first I panicked as I still had fresh memories of my childhood bedroom in my head, but as I looked around the room, I knew I was a thousand miles from the nightmare.

Not until I heard a soft, feminine giggle did I realize I had awoken to a whole new nightmare.

"Derek?" I called out, and the sound stopped as the door opened farther and Derek stepped inside with a redhead on his arm. I searched his face for some sort of answer that I already knew, but he just smiled, completely plastered.

"We need that bed," he called out, and she laughed again as they stumbled in.

"Get her out of here *now!*" I pushed to my feet and balled my fists at my sides, but my whole body shook.

"You get the fuck out." Any sign of happiness left his expression. "I paid for this room."

I was gutted.

My song still played in the background as I shoved him hard against his chest, and he stumbled, the redhead swaying, but neither fell. They laughed in my face again as he held his arm firmly around her waist and pulled her past me to the bed.

"Why would you do this? Why?" I spun around but he didn't bother to turn and look at me as he pulled his shirt over his head.

"You can't be that fucking stupid." He shook his head and finally turned to look me in the eye for a brief moment. "You barely let me touch you, Sarah. You think I was just going to live the rest of my life without—"

I couldn't take it anymore and my hand flew up and I smacked him hard across his cheek. He stared at me with murder in his eyes, but they soon went vacant and he chuckled softly as his hand rubbed over his cheek.

"It's not like this is the first time. Come on, don't look so stunned. I figured you knew. Everyone else did." He paused and met my gaze. "You know, it's funny. As close as you were to E, I'm surprised he never told you." Derek cocked his head to the side, smirking.

"He knew?"

"The whole time."

My legs were no longer able to support me; that final blow

was too much for me to handle. I turned and ran into the bath-room, slamming the door and locking it. I sank down to the floor. I had no one. There was no place for me to go. I was stuck, like my song, on repeat.

My eyes danced over the shower and I was no longer able to resist the urge to show Derek the pain that he had inflicted upon me. Maybe if he saw the fresh wounds, maybe then he would understand how much he was putting me through.

CHAPTER

Thirty-Three

ERIC

PULLED MY PILLOW over my face as I tried to drown out the sound of the banging at my door. It came again and I threw the pillow toward the door, but it fell several feet short.

"I'm sleeping!" I yelled as I rolled over in my empty bed, hating whoever had pulled me from my dreams. It was the only time I could hold her in my arms now.

"Please . . ."

I sat up at the sound of Sarah's voice. She was frantic. I rushed to the door, shrugging on my jeans as I pulled it open. She fell into my arms sobbing, her wet face against my chest. "What did he do? Did he hurt you?"

I pulled her back to examine her and realized that the wetness wasn't only from her tears. Her arms were smeared with blood, and she shook her head as she kept repeating no. I was holding on to her shoulders so tightly I knew they would probably bruise, but I couldn't bring myself to let her go.

"Tell me what he did."

She looked at me, eyes wide and frightened.

"Tell me!" I yelled, but she couldn't form words. I pushed around her and took off down the hall to Derek's room. I banged on the door, ready to bust through it if necessary.

"Get the fuck out—"

As the door opened, my fist connected with Derek's jaw with a satisfying crack. I shoved my way inside and my eyes landed on a redhead sitting on the bed, clutching a sheet to her naked body. I turned back to Derek, who lay on the ground, his neck bent against the wall in nothing but jeans.

"Get up," I said between clenched teeth.

Derek's hand was on his lip and he pulled his fingers back to examine the blood.

"What the fug you hit me for?" His words were slurred and I knew he was beyond wasted. The girl on the bed was pressing herself up against the wall in fear.

"Get dressed and get the fuck out of here now!" I pointed to her and she jumped, finding her clothes, which had been scattered around the floor. She took the sheet with her to cover her body as she slid behind me and out into the hallway. My gaze focused on Derek and all I wanted was to hurt him the way he had hurt Sarah. He had everything I ever wanted and he hurt her.

I bent down into his face so I was looking him in the eye. "You have no idea how bad you fucked up." I stood up and drew my leg back, kicking him hard in the ribs. He groaned and wrapped his arms around his waist. I took the opportunity to hit him again in the face. His nose cracked under my fist and blood covered his face. "Get on your fucking feet and fight like a goddamn man." I took a step back as I struggled to slow my breathing.

Derek was holding his nose and he pushed to his feet, standing in front of the door. I backed up a few more steps into the larger opening of the room and motioned for him to take his best shot.

"This has nothing to do with you." He spit out a mouthful of blood as he glared at me.

"This has *everything* to do with me. You had no fucking right to hurt her."

"And what? You think kicking my ass will make her fall into your arms?" He laughed and I swung, but he ducked out of my way. "She doesn't want you, E. She never did."

I wanted to make it impossible for him to smile. I lunged at him and we fell to the floor, my body landing on his and knocking the air from his lungs. His fist landed against my ribs and I hadn't anticipated the blow. I grunted and rolled off him.

He took the opening and pushed to his knees as he swung, connecting with my cheekbone. I was so angry it didn't even register. We struggled back and forth before I gained the upper hand and drove my fist into his body over and over, unleashing all of my anger on him. He had gotten the girl and he didn't even give a fuck about her. I wanted to make him hurt as much as he had hurt her. Every tear she cried would be another blow to his body. I wrapped my fingers around his throat and stared down into his empty eyes as he clawed at my arms. I didn't want to kill him. That would be too easy, but if someone didn't stop me soon, that was going to happen.

In minutes our scuffle had drawn attention from other guests. I vaguely heard Donna's voice, and soon the twins were on top of me, prying me from Derek's bloodied body. Only then did I hear Donna scream again, but she sounded so far away.

"Sarah . . ." I struggled in their grip but they held me tight. "Sarah!" I screamed, and pulled against them toward the door. They let me go, satisfied I wasn't going to try to finish off Derek, and we ran toward my room. The hall felt longer now, the walls closing in tighter as I burst through the doorway. Donna was on the floor with Sarah pulled over her lap, blood smeared from Sarah's wounds over Donna's light pink nightie. Sarah wasn't moving, and for a moment it seemed as if Donna had rocked her to sleep like a child, but when my eyes scanned the scattered pills on the floor around Sarah, I fell to my knees.

"No! No!" I shook my head as I pulled Sarah from Donna's arms and into my own lap. I ran my hand over her hair trying to wake her. The smell of her shampoo mixed with the smell of the blood turned my stomach, and tears flowed freely down my face as I held her against my chest.

Commotion was all around us but I blocked it all out as I held her against me. "You can't do this, Sarah. I take it all back. I take it back. I'll make it better. I'm so sorry. Please just wake up for me, sweetheart."

"You have to let her go. They will take care of her," Terry called out as he pulled on my arm, but I tightened my grip around her.

"Sir, you need to let her go so we can help her." A woman was bending down in front of me, and through blurred vision I could make out that she had dark hair like Sarah's. "Sir, we need you to let her go."

"Son, you need to let him go so we can help him," the medic called over my shoulder, but I refused to let my brother go. He needed me and I was just a few seconds too late. He struggled to breathe and blood gurgled in his throat; his eyes were half-open and he stared off into nothingness.

"I'm so sorry." Sobs ripped through my chest as I held his body against mine as rocks dug into my knees. My mother flew out of the front door of our house, her dress blowing back with each step. The world slowed and I studied the sadness in her eyes, a pain I had never before seen. My gaze fell to Robert as he struggled to take one last breath. My mom's feet froze and her hands flew over her mouth as she doubled over and violent sobs ripped through her body.

Then the most terrifying scream pulled from her chest. "My baby!"

My father soon followed, worry and pain on his face as his arms wrapped around my arms and he physically pulled me from my brother's lifeless body. My father slowed to a stop

*beside my mother, his eyes locked on mine. I'd never seen
such sadness and heartbreak in anyone's eyes. I felt completely helpless. I wanted to comfort my mother, to plead
with God to take me instead, but I froze, overwhelmed with
guilt.*

*"Why weren't you watching him?" My father's voice shook
and the sadness in his tone terrified me. He'd always been
such a tough man, and now with tears rolling down his face,
he was broken. "You should have been watching!"*

"Just let her go." Terry pulled on my arm again and I let it fall free
as I was swarmed by medics. They lifted her from my lap as I sat in
a daze.

Hands wrapped around my body and pulled me to my feet. I
staggered but didn't struggle as my wrists were cuffed. My eyes fell
to Donna, who still sat on the floor in shock, covered in Sarah's blood.
Someone was asking her if she had been hurt and she replied that
she was fine, but her eyes never left mine and I knew it was a lie. I had
hurt her. I swore I would do right by her and then I broke her heart.

CHAPTER Thirty-Four

SARAH

I COULDN'T GET THE taste of charcoal out of my mouth and I begged the nurse to bring me something to drink after I had purged the final contents of my stomach. They seemed to not hear me or pay me any attention as they checked my vital signs and made notes on their little pads of paper. I wanted to lash out and scream at them but I was terrified.

"I want to go home."

"Can you tell me where home is?" a balding man with wire-rim glasses asked as he pulled a pen from his pocket.

I shut my eyes tight and tried to play my song in my head, but his voice interrupted my thoughts.

"Can you tell me your name?"

"Sarah Winsor, and I don't have a home." E was my home and I had lost him.

"Why is that, Ms. Winsor?"

"I'm in a band. We travel."

"You don't have a family home? Parents?"

"No. I don't have anyone." I tried not to let that affect me, but the floodgates had already been opened and I wasn't strong enough to close them again.

"You would like to tell me where you got the pain pills and why you took them?"

I didn't know what to say, where to start.

"What about the cuts?"

"I had a headache and some guy on the street gave me the pills."

He scribbled down a few notes and adjusted his glasses on the bridge of his nose as he waited for me to continue, but I didn't say anything else.

"I would like to keep you here for a few days. We have some excellent people for you to talk to."

"No! I want to go home." I started to sit up but he put a hand on my shoulder.

"Where is home, Sarah? This is for your own good. I think you are a danger to yourself and need to be observed for a few days just to make sure you are feeling better, okay?" He smiled as if he wanted me to agree, even though I knew I had no choice in the matter.

"You can't just do that, can you? This is America. You can't just keep me here. Where is Eric? He can take care of me."

"Some friends are here to see you. I think they can help fill in some of the events that transpired for you. I'll give you some privacy."

He turned and walked out of the room as Cass and Donna came in, tears in their eyes.

"Thank God! Get me out of this place."

"Sarah, we can't . . . we can't take you out. Not yet. The doctor said . . ." Cass looked heartbroken.

"I don't care what the doctor said, Cass. I can't be here. What happened?"

Cass and Donna exchanged a look before Donna spoke up.

"Sweetie, we can fill you in on what happened, but the doctor doesn't think it is a great idea to upset you further, and they won't really tell us much about you because we aren't your family."

"You are the only family I have!" I broke down, unable to wear the mask I'd hidden behind for years. "Where is Eric?"

"Eric is in jail."

"Oh my God! They think he did this? Tell them he didn't do this! I did this! This is all my fault."

"They know." Cass put her hand on my shoulder and rubbed it gently. "He is in there for beating the hell out of Derek."

I sagged back against the bed as I let that sink in. "What will I do here all by myself?"

Another look passed between them before Donna cleared her throat.

"They contacted your family. Someone is coming."

"No." I shook my head. "You can't let them come."

"It's done, sweetie." Cass shook her head as a tear fell. I had never told her the truth of my past, but I could see in her eyes that she understood. I nodded, swallowing back the nasty charcoal they had given me to induce vomiting.

The doctor returned, tucking his pen in the breast pocket of his white coat. "I think we should let her get some rest for a while." He smiled at Donna and Cass and they nodded, giving me an apologetic smile before hurrying out of the curtained room.

CHAPTER
Thirty-Five

ERIC

I DIDN'T DESERVE TO be here but would gladly do it all over again. I squeezed the dark bars in front of me until my knuckles turned white and my palms threatened to bleed, layers of paint chipping and sticking to my damp palms. The minutes felt like hours and my skin began to crawl with the waiting.

I was informed that Derek had pulled through his beating, and I was partially relieved. I didn't want to spend my life in prison, but if it kept him from hurting Sarah again, I would gladly take my last breath in this cell if it meant that she was finally free from her emotional hell.

I hadn't received any word about her condition and it was killing me. I paced the floor endlessly, refusing to sleep or eat until I knew if she was safe. It was probably the only thing keeping me alive right now. I needed to know she was safe. That was all that mattered.

Minutes ticked by like hours. The greatest way to torture a man is to leave him alone with his own thoughts. I counted the cinder blocks that made up the walls and I sang every song we wrote, but none of it seemed to pass the time.

I was in a holding cell by myself so I didn't even have the luxury of someone to talk to. It was maddening.

"You want to end up in jail?" My dad was on his second case of beer and he only got meaner with each can.

"Like you care. At least then I will have some peace. I could go the rest of my life without seeing the blame on your eyes." I stalked off to my room, hating that he was killing my buzz.

"You ungrateful little shit!" he yelled after me, and I heard him put down the footrest of his recliner.

I turned around in the hall, preparing for the beating that was sure to follow. But my father just covered his face as he began to cry and shoved past me to his room. Somehow it was worse and I wished he would have hit me. I didn't like to see everyone around me suffering because of what I had done.

CHAPTER Thirty-Six

SARAH

I WAS LOCKED IN a cage like a little bird. The room was sterile but somehow felt dirty. I was on the fifth floor of the hospital, a floor reserved for those who needed rest. *Needing rest* was code for "crazy," but it was nice that they tried to spare my feelings. I didn't want to rest, I wanted to run as far away from here as possible.

"Can you tell me what you're feeling right now, Sarah?" the woman next to me asked, and I couldn't help but laugh as I cried. What a silly question. I was locked up against my will with cuts slicing down my arms and I had just been forced to vomit up the handful of pills I had swallowed. How did she think I felt?

"Why are you asking me such a stupid question?" I looked toward the far wall as I tried not to focus on the panic that had settled in my chest.

"Why do you think it is stupid?"

"Who is coming to visit me?" I turned to look her in the eye now.

"No one if we don't think it will be conducive to your recovery. But we can't be sure of that without getting some answers from you." She leaned close and placed her hand on top of mine. "We want to help. We can't do that without you wanting it. Aren't you tired, Sarah? Tired of holding it all in until it explodes like it did today?"

I closed my eyes, taking a deep breath as I begged my body to stop shaking. I couldn't do this anymore. I was tired of pretending to be strong until I hurt myself. The sooner I cooperated, the sooner I could move on with my life.

"I was eleven when my mom married Phil."

The memories, the nightmares, all poured out of me. I told her about my shame and guilt. I even told her how I had left my little sister behind in that hellhole.

She never judged me or told me I was a bad person, even when I explained the events that had led me to this place.

I expected looks of disgust but was met with sympathy, and I wished I had met her years ago, but I knew in a place such as this my story was probably something she had heard a million times over. I'm sure she was desensitized to it all, and I wished I could be. I hated how heavy my chest felt as I thought of those nights.

After our talk I was given my dinner and told that I should participate in a group meeting. The idea made me panic all over again. I could stand in front of thousands and pour out my soul, but somehow this was worse. I would have to look others in the eye as I confessed my sins. I didn't want to be judged by my peers. I wanted to be the Sarah who was onstage. She was a fearless rock star that people loved, but it was all smoke and mirrors.

I barely managed to keep anything down, and that the hospital food sucked didn't help. I ate half of my Salisbury steak and pushed my vegetable mix and mashed potatoes around my tray.

The nurse eased my fears about the meeting as we walked down the narrow, white hallway and into a large common area.

"This won't be very painful, I promise. This is an anger management group."

"Oh . . . I'm not angry." I stopped walking and shook my head.

She smiled over at me and put her hand on my back to urge me forward. "We're all angry, sweet pea." She winked. "We just need to know the right ways to deal with it."

The room had hotel-type couches and a few games stacked along one of the walls. I expected the patients to be crazy and climbing the walls, but I was surprised to find that most looked like me.

I stopped in the doorway, covering the bandages on my one arm with my hand, feeling embarrassed. "I'm cold. Can I get a sweater?"

The nurse smiled at me, her hand rubbing over my back the way a mother would caress a child. "You can't hide from your problems. They don't go away like that." She glanced over the handful of patients lounging on the couches. "They all have a story to tell, just like you. Don't be scared."

I nodded, pulling my lower lip between my teeth as I slowly walked over to an empty spot on a couch. I kept my eyes downcast as a few of the others talked among themselves. I pulled my legs up to my chest as I pulled a strand of hair in front of my face and inspected it for split ends. I needed something, anything, to keep my focus off the situation. "Free Bird" played loudly in my head as I tried to use my oldest method of escape, but it wasn't working. I could feel everyone's eyes on me, and I wanted to run back to my room and lock myself inside, even though I was sure the doors didn't have locks, at least not on the inside.

Finally, an older gentleman who looked like someone's grandpa came in and took a seat in a wingback chair. He wore a button-down shirt with a gray-and-maroon sweater vest and dark gray slacks.

"Welcome, everyone. For those of you that are new to the

group, my name is Dr. Rodgers, but I like to keep it friendly, so you can call me Phil."

My skin began to crawl at the mention of his name. I peeled one of the pieces of medical tape from my bandage and scratched my nails over one of my cuts.

"This is an anger management group. We are going to discuss healthy ways to deal with anger, but first, let's introduce ourselves, shall we?" He smiled wide as his eyes danced around the group.

"I'm Jake," said a boy who looked about eighteen or nineteen, shrugging his overgrown brown hair from his eyes.

"Would you like to share something about yourself with the group, Jake?"

"Yeah. This group is fucking pointless."

Dr. Rodgers nodded and folded his hands on his lap. "Dually noted, Jake."

"My name is Annie. I'm fifteen and I don't belong here," a young girl with shoulder-length blond hair said. Her voice reminded me of a cartoon character's and she looked like one of those overly popular girls from school. She didn't look as if she belonged here at all.

"Excellent, Annie. Stick around and participate and we will see how it fits for you."

She rolled her eyes as the doctor spoke, and I hated how blatantly disrespectful she was to him.

"I'm Joel and I *know* I need this group." The room erupted in laughter at the boy in his early twenties with his hair buzzed to the scalp. He looked as if he belonged in an army barracks somewhere and not in a nuthouse.

"Don't we all know it, Joel." The doctor chuckled and it reminded me of Santa Claus.

All eyes turned to me and I stiffened as I tried not to meet their gazes. "My name is Sarah."

"Nice to meet you, Sarah." The doctor smiled.

"Nice to meet you, too, Dr. Rodgers."

"Please, call me Phil."

Bile rose in my throat and I dragged my nail over one of my cuts again, focusing on that pain as opposed to that in my chest.

"I'd rather not." I ground my teeth together as I spoke, trying not to let my voice shake.

His eyes drifted down to my bandage, which now had a fresh spot of red around the corner. "You can call me whatever you like." His smile was back in place but I knew he had seen what I had done. "Would you like to share something about yourself?"

I glanced around at all the faces as they waited patiently for me to say something. "I . . . like to sing."

"Perfect. You are the only one who had something positive to say. That's very good, Sarah."

I gave him a halfhearted smile and he focused his attention on the group as a whole. I relaxed in my seat.

AFTER A SLEEPLESS night I was sent to meet with a therapist. I was asked a million questions but most had to be repeated as I slipped inside my head and began tapping out the beat to one of my songs. I wished I had finished my song with E. I wished I had done so many things, but ending up in a place like this felt unavoidable. I still couldn't see a way out.

"I'd like to get you started on a few prescriptions, but to be honest with you, Sarah, the true healing will come from therapy."

"Can you tell me how my boyfriend is doing?" Even after all he had done, I couldn't help but worry about him. If I could force my heart to forget him, I would. But I knew that would only come with time.

She flipped through the papers on her desk as she read over them. "Can you tell me the events that lead to your stay with us?"

"I already told that other lady." I rolled my eyes and the therapist took off her glasses and sat them on her desk as she relaxed in her chair. I didn't like that she was talking to me as if I were a child.

"I have her notes, but I'd like to hear it from you."

"You have her notes?" I pushed up from my oversize chair, feeling betrayed.

"Sarah, we are all here to help you. We can't do that if you won't open up and trust us."

"I did open up, once, but apparently I trusted too soon. I want to go home." I folded my arms over my chest and the doctor pressed her lips together in a tight line as her gaze fell to my bloodied bandage.

"Where is home?"

"I don't know. I need to talk to Derek. I need to make sure he is okay. He could be dead for all I know, and none of you will tell me anything."

"Derek was released this morning. He was bruised and needed a few stitches, but nothing was broken."

I sat back down in my seat as the wind was knocked out of me. "I want to see him. I want him to come visit me." I peeled the remainder of the paint from my thumbnail. I needed to show him what he did, what all of his lying and cheating had done to the person he was supposed to love.

"He flew to Texas to be with his family. I'm sorry, Sarah. I wanted to bring him in on one of our sessions but he didn't want to participate."

It felt like a shotgun blast to the chest. He had left me? After what he had done and the things he had said, *he* left *me*?

He didn't even care enough to find out if I was okay?

CHAPTER
Thirty-Seven

ERIC

"ERIC WALKER, LET'S go." The guard unlocked the gate to my cell and took a step back. I nodded to him as I walked through, feeling the pressure in my chest ease slightly. "Time for your arraignment."

I followed behind the guard as we made our way to the small courthouse that was in the same building as the little jail. I didn't care what the judge had to say. I had given up years ago and was just living on borrowed time. That was more clear to me now than ever.

It was nice getting out of the cramped space, and I hoped I wouldn't have to spend much more time in there without knowing how Sarah was doing.

I had been thinking about the moment when I could see her again and if I should. What I had done was selfish, but I had never meant to hurt her. I only wanted to make her happy. The look on Donna's face as they placed me in handcuffs also haunted my memories.

I'd managed to kill two birds with one stone.

I BARELY REGISTERED anything the judge said. All I could think about was Sarah. No one would tell me anything and I was dying with each passing second, not knowing if she was safe. I was ordered to do community service, and since Derek declined to press charges, the punishment was just a slap on the wrist. I guess I was lucky, but a part of me had almost wanted them to lay the hammer down, to make me pay for all that I'd done. To everyone.

I was taken back to the small holding cell as the paperwork was processed, and I would soon get to walk. My skin was beginning to crawl with anticipation and fear. I didn't know where I would go from here.

I didn't know what to expect when the guard opened the gate and motioned for me to exit the cell. He led me down a narrow corridor and through several sets of doors. Donna stood on the other side, and I wanted to wrap my arms around her. It was so good to see a familiar face. She smiled sadly and looked to the guard before her gaze dropped to her hands.

"I took care of what I could for you."

I took a step forward but she held up a hand to stop me as she inhaled audibly. "I know why you did it."

"He deserved it after what he did to her." I closed my eyes as I struggled not to let my anger show.

Donna shook her head. "You can't blame yourself for her choices. She knew what kind of person he was and she chose to deny it. You can't save her from herself, E. She needs to do that herself." Donna's eyes locked on mine. She was sad but confident in her words. "I didn't tell you about my past to make you feel guilty. I told you because you were my friend and I cared about you."

"Were?"

"I will always care about you, E. More than you will ever know. But I won't be second choice."

"I choose you."

She laughed quietly as her teeth dragged over her lower lip. "You know what I love about you? You try so hard to fight against everything inside of you and to do the right thing, but you can't change what is in your heart. It was always her for you and it didn't matter who or what stood in the way of that." Donna's face was somber now.

"There was a time you told me that you loved *everything* about me."

"Yeah . . ." She stared down at her shoes.

I nodded and ran my hand through my hair. I was completely alone now, but it was for the best. I wouldn't hurt anyone else.

"Is she . . ." I couldn't even say the words. I was a coward. If I was responsible for her death, I couldn't go on.

"She is going to be okay. She is getting the help she needs. It seems she was given the pills by some stranger on the street." Donna raised her eyebrows, knowing damn well the pills were mine.

I nodded, unable to look her in the eye. I knew I shouldn't be asking her about Sarah, and I knew that all of this was my fault. I could have gone to a doctor to refill my prescription, but our schedule never kept me in one place long enough to keep an appointment, and I didn't like reliving my past with each new doctor I saw.

"They are keeping her for a few days just to make sure she is okay. They contacted her family and they are coming to take care of her."

"Her family? No. She can't see them." I felt as if I were going to be sick.

"It's too late."

"What happens now?" I hung my head as the sharp, familiar pain of one of my headaches took over, but I didn't want any relief. I deserved to suffer.

"I'm going to go back home and work out some of my own problems. It's time to stop running away." Her eyes danced over me one last time before she turned and pushed through the door behind her.

"Let's go. We need to outprocess and then you will be free to go."

I PUSHED OUT of the front door, the sunlight blinding me as I walked toward the curb on the other side of the parking lot. A bus ran every half hour. The air was warm and pleasant. Under any other circumstance I would have been smiling, but as the bus pulled up in front of me, I couldn't find a reason to smile.

I stepped inside and paid the fair before taking an empty seat near the back. I stared out of the window as we pulled away from the curb. I thought it would feel good to be free again, but I would never truly be free. I was carrying the weight of my past on my shoulders and I was tired.

I needed to do something to make all of this right. I could never make it up to my brother, but with Sarah I still had a chance.

I rode the bus north until it didn't go any farther. I got out, glancing around the unfamiliar street.

"Can you tell me where the closest hospital is?" I asked an elderly woman who sat on the bench in front of me, waiting for the next bus to come.

CHAPTER

Thirty-Eight

SARAH

I TRIED TO ESCAPE from my thoughts, but it was use-less. A knock came at the door to my room and I turned to see a nurse standing in the open space.

"You have a visitor."

I pushed up from my bed, terrified and hopeful in the same moment. The nurse stepped aside to reveal a woman who looked like the mirror image of myself, only younger. I blinked, unable to believe what I was seeing.

"Jenny?" I pushed to my feet and my vision blurred. I wanted to run toward her, embrace her, but I stopped. I hadn't spoken to her in years and she had every right to hate me. But then she took a step forward and then lunged toward me, wrapping her arms around me and pulling me against her.

"I'm so sorry, Jenny. I'm so sorry," I whispered over and over as she buried her face in the crook of my neck. "I shouldn't have left you there with him. I'll never forgive myself." I pulled back to look her in the eye.

She grabbed my hands and squeezed them tightly as tears streamed down her cheeks. "No. Don't do this. I was safe. I went and lived with Aunt Carla."

Relief washed over me as I realized she had never had to endure what I went through. I had been carrying around the guilt of what could have happened for years, and it had slowly been killing me.

"Why didn't you go to her house, Sarah? Why didn't you ever come find me?"

"I couldn't look you in the eye after . . . after what had happened. I was afraid everyone blamed me . . . afraid of what had happened after I'd left you . . . I couldn't face it."

"No one blamed you. Not even Mom. She was devastated by what happened."

"What?" Jenny knew? And she told Mom? And Mom was . . . devastated? Maybe her indifference to my pain had just been . . . blindness?

All of these years I thought I carried the burden of this secret alone.

"When you didn't come meet me at school, I knew you had finally left. I ran back in and told my teacher to call Mom at work. I didn't understand. I was too young back then, but I knew you ran away because of Phil. I tried to explain it to Mom. She wasn't sure what had happened, but she knew it had to be more than you just disliking him." She paused and met my gaze. "She confronted him and he denied ever doing anything to you, but she knew he couldn't be trusted to be around me without knowing the whole story. She took me to Carla's and we never went back. She tried to have Phil arrested, but without you there wasn't any proof, and all I knew was that he scared you and was always trying to be alone with you when Mom wasn't around."

I took a few steps back and sank down on the edge of the bed as my thoughts raced with all of this new information. Everyone knew. I could have told my mother . . .and she would have believed me. Jenny had been safe all this time.

"How did you know I was here? How did they find you?"

"You have some very good friends that really care about you. Cass spent hours scouring the Internet, Facebook, everything. It was her who got in touch with us."

"How is Mom?"

"She misses you."

"Then why isn't she here?"

"She blames herself for what happened to you, Sarah. It nearly killed her, you know. She was afraid you wouldn't want to see her." She swallowed. "She's never stopped thinking about you, talking about you . . . She's just been living in fear that you hate her, that you blame her like she blames herself . . ."

"That makes two of us." I looked over my sister. She was wearing a sundress with yellow roses covering the bottom of the skirt. She wore little makeup and her hair was swept up in a ponytail.

The nurse who had been waiting in the hallway stepped inside, clearing her throat. "Are you okay, Sarah?" Her eyes danced between my sister and me.

"Yeah, I think . . . I think that, finally, I am."

CHAPTER

Thirty-Nine

ERIC

NEED TO SEE Sarah Winsor."

"Are you family?" the receptionist asked as she clicked the keys on her computer. She glanced up at me, her eyes inspecting the injuries to my hands from beating the hell out of Derek. "It looks like she has a visitor right now and she is under restriction."

"Who? Who is here to see her?" I leaned over the desk toward her.

"You need to lower your voice, sir. I can't divulge that information to you. You will have to wait to see her when she is released."

"When will that be?"

"I don't know, sir. That is up to her doctor. I'm sorry."

I slammed my hands down on the counter before stalking off and out the front door of the hospital. I paced back and forth on the sidewalk as I tried to figure out what to do next. She was so close and I couldn't protect her. How could they call her family? What if her stepdad was up there with her right now?

I wanted to fight my way to her, but I had no idea where in the building she was. All I could do was wait for this torture to end and hope whatever she was enduring wasn't going to be the final straw that broke her completely.

I sank down on the sidewalk and leaned back against the hospital wall as I stared out at the clouds overhead. People came and went, some filled with joy at the start of a new life, others in tears as a life had ended.

As I watched, it seemed as if the world had stopped for each of them, nothing more important than this moment. Some prayed, others cursed, and I sat there, helpless as the rest. It hit me that I was still imprisoned, even if I wasn't behind bars.

The automatic doors slid open beside me and my heart stopped as a brunette walked by me and into the street. I pushed to my feet and took off after her.

"Sarah?" I yelled, and put my hand on her shoulder. As she turned to face me, she looked startled. Her resemblance to Sarah was unbelievable. She was what I imagined Sarah would look like had she not been through hell. "Jenny?" I asked as I recalled Sarah's confessions about her little sister, whom she had left behind.

"Are you Derek?" She took a step back from me.

"No. Wait. He isn't with her?"

"I need to know who you are before I tell you anything about my sister."

"I'm E. I know she probably doesn't want to see me." My head pounded and I tried to swallow the pain.

"She told me what you did for her. Thank you. It's good to know someone was looking out for her. All this time I thought she was alone."

"Someone had to after her family abandoned her," I snapped, immediately regretting my words. Jenny was only a child when Sarah left and it wasn't her fault.

"Do you want to go for a coffee or something so we can talk a little more privately?" She leaned her head toward the parking lot.

"I need to wait here for Sarah."

"They plan to release her tomorrow. There is nothing you can do until then. She's going to be okay."

I nodded reluctantly and she turned to continue walking toward her car, and I followed her to an old, brown Volkswagen Beetle.

We rode in silence as the radio played upbeat pop music. I couldn't help but laugh and shake my head.

"What? This is a good song."

"You are nothing like your sister." Even thinking of Sarah was painful and I stared out the window, the smile falling from my face.

"Tell me about her."

"First, I need to know about your parents."

Jenny glanced over at me, not sure of what she could say or what I already knew.

"Sarah told me everything. *Everything.*"

"It's not what you think. She was scared. She didn't think anyone would help her. We had no idea where she had gone when she ran away."

"Why isn't her mother here if she was so worried after Sarah left? Why didn't she go after her?"

"She still hasn't forgiven herself for what happened."

"Good. I haven't forgiven her either."

Jenny sighed as she clicked on her turn signal and turned down another road. "She didn't know. When she found out, she left Phil." Jenny's eyes met mine briefly as I absorbed that new information.

"Sarah is a singer." I smiled as I relaxed my head against the seat. "Her band toured with mine."

"Was Derek in her band?"

I shook my head, not wanting to explain how things fell apart with Derek. That was Sarah's story to tell. "Where is he?"

"Sarah said he went to Texas."

When Sarah needed him most, he had abandoned her once again. He was lucky he was so far away or I would have hunted his ass down and finished what I had started.

"She was supposed to go with him." I clenched my jaw as I re-membered how much it had killed me when I had found that out.

"I want her to come stay with me for a while. She needs to be with family."

CHAPTER Forty

SARAH

"YOU SEEM TO be in better spirits."

I glanced up at Cass, who sat cross-legged on the end of my bed. "I saw my sister for the first time since I had left home."

"How did you feel about seeing her after all of these years?"

"Terrified."

"And now?"

"Relieved. Thank you for finding her."

"Change isn't always a bad thing, you know."

"It usually is for me."

"What you are going to do when you leave here?"

"I don't know what I am going to do. I'm pretty sure I no

longer have a band." I laughed sadly as I thought about Derek. "I'm sure everyone thinks I am crazy." I heard E's voice in my mind telling me I was killing him. I wanted to tell him then what he meant to me, but it was too late. Every person I got close to ran from me eventually.

"You are hardly the crazy one in our messed-up family."

I pictured Cass and Tucker looking at each other with love in their eyes. They had been through so much together and now their lives were perfect. I wondered if it would ever be possible to get past everything and one day be happy like them.

"My boyfriend ran off to Texas and left me here, and E . . ." I hated how my heart ached as I thought of him.

"Do you miss him?" Cass pulled her lip between her teeth.

"So much . . . and now he is sitting in jail because of me."

"I was talking about Derek."

I could feel my cheeks flush and I looked down at the pillow on my lap, picking a loose thread with my nails. "I knew he was no good for me, but he was always there and he never asked questions."

"It's always way easier to deny anything had happened than face it." Cass paused and glanced down at her hands. "I can relate to that."

"Something like that, I guess." I nodded, knowing she understood better than anyone else.

"But the problems didn't go away that way, did they?"

"I'm here aren't I?" I joked, trying to hide behind my humor.

"But you told E. You could have talked to me."

"He cared."

"We all care about you, Sarah. I know we have been crazy busy with touring and getting married, but I would have been there for you."

"E deserves so much better than me."

"And you deserved to be cheated on, humiliated . . . cast aside?"

I didn't say anything as I shifted on the bed. I didn't want to talk about E anymore.

"In here it is easy to avoid what is bothering you, but tomorrow you are going to be out there again and you can't run forever. Trust me. I tried that once."

THE DOCTOR LOOKED over the cuts on my arms. I was slowly starting to heal, both inside and out. As scared as I was to leave this place, I was going stir-crazy after four days of this. I wanted to see Jenny again and find out everything about her life since I had left.

"You're all set. Take care of yourself." He patted me on the shoulder as I slid off the chair and walked back to my room.

As I changed into my street clothes, the nurse popped her head into my room with a bright smile on her face. "Your sister is here for you. I have her waiting down the hall at the front desk."

"Thank you." I smiled. I glanced around the sterile space and took a deep breath before heading out into the hallway. Jenny's eyes met mine and she ran down the hall toward me, pulling me in for a hug.

"I missed you," she said, and I pulled back as I tucked my hair behind my ear. It was overwhelming. She looped her arm in mine and began walking with me down the hall to the double doors. "Come on. I have someone waiting for you." I stopped walking, unsure if I could handle seeing my mom yet. I had run off, no explanation, and she had no idea if I was even alive for all of this time. "It's going to be fine. I promise you. I'm with you now."

I slowly began to walk again. The nurse who stood by the doors slid his card so they would open, and we made our way to the elevator. The doors opened and a nurse stepped out as we slid in and pressed the button for the first floor.

CHAPTER

Forty-One

ERIC

T HIS ISN'T YOUR fault." Cass leaned back against the wall next to me as I stared at Tuck and the twins.

"I just need to take some time off." I flexed my hands, my fingers still throbbing from my fight with Derek.

The doors opened in front of us and we all stopped talking as our eyes fell on Sarah and her sister, Jenny.

Sarah looked completely shocked, her eyes wide, but Jenny was smiling at all of us. They stepped forward, their arms linked together.

Cass flew forward, wrapping her arms around Sarah as they both laughed.

"I am so glad you are okay," Cass whispered, and kissed Sarah on the cheek.

"I didn't think you guys would be here," Sarah said, and I took a deep breath, not realizing how much I had missed the sound of her voice. I stood there just watching as everyone hugged her and told her how much they'd missed her.

Eventually the conversation died down and her eyes met mine. Everyone took notice.

"We'll wait out at the car," Cass said as she placed her hand on Sarah's shoulder, then all the guys but me followed Cass toward the front doors.

"You okay?" Jenny asked, and Sarah nodded, her eyes still on me. Jenny followed the others, leaving only Sarah and me.

She took a step closer and I stayed against the wall, my hands shoved in my pockets.

"I didn't think I would see you again," she said shakily.

"I'm so sorry, Sarah." I shook my head as I swallowed down the lump in my throat.

"I'm the one who should be sorry. I put you through a lot of shit."

I laughed as I thought over how much we had been through the past week. "I'm just glad you're okay."

"Are *you* okay?"

"I am now." I wanted to reach out and wrap my arms around her, but I forced myself not to move. "I thought you . . ." I cleared my throat as I tried not to relive the feelings of helplessness when I didn't know if she was even alive.

"I'm sorry," she whispered, and took another step closer.

"Hey, I've gotten to meet Jenny. She's a lot like you, but her taste in music sucks," I joked, and Sarah smiled. God I loved to see her smile.

"We will have to fix that."

It didn't slip by me that she had said *we*.

"The world is waiting." I pushed from the wall and began walking toward the front door with Sarah at my side.

Jenny was waiting just outside the doors, leaning against her car. The band was standing around a dark SUV parked in front of her.

I blew out a heavy breath and turned to Sarah. I hated spending a second away from her, but I knew what she needed right now was her family. Jenny and I had talked for hours about Sarah's life, and I knew I had to do what was best for her, not me.

"Don't party too hard," I said with a smile that I knew didn't reach my eyes.

"You're not coming with me?"

I shook my head and she wrapped her arms around my neck. I slowly let mine circle her body, not sure if I would ever be able to let her go.

"Please don't leave me, too," she whispered against my ear, and I stiffened, hating myself for having to walk away.

Tucker's hand landed on my shoulder and he pulled me back. I reluctantly let go of Sarah and watched as her sister opened the car door for her to get in.

"Come on, man. She'll be fine," Chris said, then through the windshield of her sister's car I watched Sarah fasten her seat belt.

CHAPTER Forty-Two

SARAH

THERE WERE NO words to describe the pain of watching E get in his car and pull away. I was left with a virtual stranger. Jenny grabbed my hand and gave it a reassuring squeeze before pulling out onto the road.

"Mom is really excited to see you," she said as I reached out to turn off the annoying pop music that blared through the speakers. I found a station playing classic rock and turned up the volume to let Jenny know I didn't feel like talking.

My entire world had changed so quickly I didn't even know who I was anymore. I didn't have a boyfriend or a band. Suddenly, I had my family back . . . and E was gone.

We drove for nearly three hours and only stopped to get

gas and a bite to eat. I didn't say a word to Jenny, but she didn't seem to mind the silence between us.

We turned off on a tree-lined street with small, two-story houses lining the way. The car slowed and pulled off in front of a pale blue home with white shutters. I looked over at Jenny.

She smiled brightly at me. "It's going to be fine. I promise."

I nodded and she slipped out of the driver's side as I opened my door and pushed to my feet. I groaned and stretched as I stared at the house.

Jenny came to my side and linked her arm in mine as she had at the hospital. "Come on."

I reluctantly walked toward the front door and waited for Jenny to open it and step inside.

"Mom?" she called out as I followed her in. The house was small but clean, and the walls were lined with pictures. My eyes danced over then as I examined how sad I had looked as a child.

"Jenny, have you brought her home?" a familiar voice called from another room, and I clamped my hand over my mouth to keep from crying out. I hadn't realized how much I had missed my mother until I heard her voice for the first time in too many years.

"Come on." Jenny's eyes lit up and she headed down a narrow hallway. She paused at a closed door and looked to me before pushing it open.

As I stepped inside, my eyes scanned the bedroom. It was pale pink and the curtains were white lace. The sun shone through the curtains, covering the walls with a crazy shadowy pattern. My eyes fell to the bed, with a matching pink blanket, and my mother propped up with pillows. She looked so much older, and almost frail. She was bedridden from a bad case of the flu. Jenny said my mother's health had deteriorated over the years, but it didn't prepare me for seeing her, once so beautiful and active, now so much older and weak.

"Mom?" I could barely hear my own voice.

"I've missed you so much, Sarah." She held out her arms and I ran to her, overwhelmed by too many emotions, falling over her chest as I hugged her and cried happy tears for the first time since I could remember.

"I'm sorry, Mom."

"I'm so sorry, too . . . so sorry." She was sobbing as well. "But why didn't you come home? You could have always come home, Sarah."

Then her eyes danced over the red lines that marred my arms.

"I was scared. I didn't know Phil was gone. I didn't know if you would believe me. I figured you would want me gone anyway when you found out. . . . I felt guilty, like I had done something wrong." My voice trailed off.

"You didn't do anything wrong." She put her hands on my cheeks and looked straight into my eyes. "I thought all this time you blamed me. Sarah, you and Jenny mean more to me than the world. I would have protected you, sweet girl. I swear I had no idea."

"I know you didn't, and I didn't ever blame you. I just didn't know how to deal with everything, so I ran."

"I tried to find you, but after a while the police assumed you . . . that something had happened. You didn't make it easy. Without credit cards or anything of that nature, you had just vanished."

"I thought about coming home so many times, but I didn't know that Phil was gone, and after a while I couldn't look you in the eye after just leaving like that. I know I put you through hell. I'm so sorry for all of this."

"It's okay now. I have you back."

"I'm so sorry for leaving you, Mom."

"Life is too short. I'm just thankful for today." She pulled me down against her and Jenny's arms slid over my back as she joined our hug.

CHAPTER
Forty-Three

ERIC

"YOU SURE ABOUT this?" Tuck asked me for the hundredth time. I rolled my eyes as I grabbed Sarah's guitar. The guys had packed up all my belongings from my room and moved them to a new hotel after the incident.

"You know I am."

"We support you no matter what you decide to do, but it won't be the same without you."

"It's only a few months. I'll be back in time for the next tour."

Cass made sure I had all of my belongings before we said our good-byes. "Don't forget about us," she said as she hugged me.

"Not possible," I replied as I hugged each of the twins.

"Stay out of trouble," Tuck said with a laugh.

"I'll do my best, but no promises."

I looked at the band one last time before I turned and left. This escape was long overdue. I dumped my bags into the back of my waiting rental car and pulled off into traffic. I pulled out my new cell phone that I had picked up yesterday and flipped through the contacts. I found Jenny's number and typed out a quick text as I stopped at a red light.

How did it go?
She's handling it well. She misses you.

I tossed my phone on the dash as traffic began to move and cranked up the radio. I had my own healing to do and I needed to start getting my life together if I ever wanted to have a future with someone else.

I DROVE FOR hours, not stopping to sleep until my eyes burned and I could no longer focus. I pulled off at an old truck stop and slept in the driver's seat of the car until the sun blinded me through the windshield. I sat up, groaning as I watched people walking in and out of the gas station.

I pulled back out onto the highway and continued on my trip across the country. I only stopped for food and fuel, burning away the daylight.

As night fell, I finally allowed myself to think about Sarah. I had been trying to push her from my thoughts. It was too painful. As fucked-up as this trip had been, she was finally in a better place in her life. I hoped to be able to get myself to that point as well. I had carried demons with me for too many years. I wanted to move on and finally be able to be happy. That would start with confronting the past. If Sarah could do it, so could I.

I stared off at my house in eastern Tennessee. The yard now had a stone border around it at least three feet high. I could still see it as it was that day my brother was killed. I got out of the car and walked up to the edge of the property as the front door opened. My mother stood in the entrance with her hand over her mouth as if she had just seen a ghost.

"Mike!" she called over her shoulder, and my father soon appeared behind her. I walked around the stone wall and slowly made my way up the driveway. My mother practically fell down the steps as she ran to meet me. I lifted her in the air as I held her, my eyes slowly opening and landing on my father. He nodded and I returned the gesture as I set my mother back down.

"Are you here to stay?" she asked excitedly.

I couldn't help but laugh. "No, Ma. I have things to handle in California. I'm just here for a visit." I didn't need to tell them about my community service. This was more for closure and not to catch up.

"Son," my dad said with another nod. He had lost weight, but he didn't look as healthy. I guess years of carrying around guilt will do that to you.

"Let's get you something to eat. Are you hungry?" my mother asked as she made her way to the front door.

"I could eat," I said, and followed her inside.

WE TALKED FOR hours as I told my mother about the band and how much my life had changed. She seemed genuinely proud, and even my father didn't have anything rude to say about my career choice.

Afterward I went down the hallway and pushed open the door to my brother's room. It looked as if it hadn't been touched since that day, but not a speck of dust was to be found, so I knew my mother spent a lot of time in there.

"It never gets easier," my father said from behind me. I nodded but didn't respond. He was right. Instead of accepting what had happened, I'd carried the guilt around with me like a scarlet letter, keeping myself from being able to move past it.

"I am sorry."

"It wasn't your fault. I know you probably don't want to hear anything from me, but I had thought about this moment for years. When you left, I realized what I had done. I pushed you away as I drowned in my own grief. I never realized how much grief *you* carried. I didn't make life easy on you. After you didn't come home, we had to mourn the loss of both our sons. I deserved it. I know that, but your mother . . ." He shook his head as he ran his hand over his forehead. "You can't run out on her again. She won't be able to take it."

I nodded, knowing he was right. Mom hadn't deserved what I put her through. She had no more control over my dad than I did.

"I couldn't stay." I swallowed against the lump that had formed in my throat.

"No one blames you. Not for what happened and not for leaving."

My eyes met his. The sadness I had seen on that painful day now filled his eyes again. All these years I thought he hadn't loved me. All these years I carried the burden of being the one who should have died. That painful guilt began to ease from my chest as I looked into his eyes.

"I should have saved him." I shook my head, begging the tears not to fall.

"Is that why you wanted to join the army? You wanted to make up for not saving him?"

"Maybe." I shrugged and ran my hand over my hair as I took a deep breath. "Or I would have died trying. I know it wouldn't have brought him back, but it was the only way I could make things right."

My father took a heavy step toward me, his body crashing into mine as he shook. His arms wrapped around my shoulders and I squeezed my eyes closed as the tears fell from my lashes. I slowly raised my arms and wrapped them around my father's back, a moment years overdue.

"I was a shitty father and a shitty husband."

"You're only human, Dad." For years I had built my father up to be a monster, but I knew now that he didn't know how to handle his grief. It didn't excuse the past, but it was something we could work forward from and I wanted that more than anything. He patted my back hard as he pulled back from our embrace.

"I am *glad* you are my son." His voice was barely a whisper as he struggled to contain his composure. He turned and left the room without another word.

But for now, that was enough. It was all I needed to start to be able to heal. I closed my brother's door and made my way into my bedroom. It looked frozen in time. I grabbed my football from the dresser and tossed it in my hands as my eyes scanned an old corkboard that hung on the wall. It was full of drawings I had done over the years. The walls were still pea green, but it looked as if someone had repainted them over the years. My eyes danced over the rock posters that lined the walls, and I had to laugh at how much my taste in music had changed over the years. I pushed up the window behind my bed to let some fresh air in, a window that I had used to sneak out more times than I could count.

I pulled my phone from my pocket and sent Cass a text.

In the twilight zone.

How is it going?

I'll live.

I shoved my phone back in my pocket and lay down on my bed, finally letting my exhaustion take over. I knew things with my family were far from fixed, but I was no longer going to run from my problems. It was time to be a man. Being in jail and watching Sarah nearly die had put everything in perspective for me. Being her friend had given me someone to share my problems with, but it was more than that. She gave me the courage to face my past and hope for the future. I wanted to live up to the person she saw when she looked at me. She had no idea how much I appreciated having her in my life. I hated when she left after the tour, but I was willing to let her go and try to move on if she was happy. After she came back, it made me realize that not only hadn't things changed in her life, but I didn't ever want her to leave again. It killed me inside to see her world spiral out of control and not be able to stop it all from crashing down.

I wouldn't let her down again, I couldn't. She needed me now as much as I needed her. My next breath whispered her name and my heart beat to the sound of our song.

I was completely and un-fucking-believably in love with her.

CHAPTER

Forty-Four

SARAH

I'D FALLEN INTO a routine with my sister and mom over the last two weeks. I took over grocery shopping because Jenny sucked at it and I didn't think I could live off mac and cheese for too much longer. My mom needed something healthier anyway.

After I returned to the house from the grocery store today, I began to cook dinner. I didn't know how to make much so I stuck with spaghetti. Jenny said she was going to invite a friend over so I made two boxes, which turned out to be a ridiculous amount of food.

Mom was out of bed and feeling better after a bad case of the flu. She helped roll out meatballs and talked about life as if I had only stepped out for a day. It was nice feeling that I belonged somewhere, but I still missed my friends.

"That smells amazing!" Jenny grabbed her purse and headed for the front door.

"It is, and if you don't have your ass back here when it is done, you don't get any!" I called after her.

"Watch your mouth! You may be an adult but I am still your mother!" My mom smirked.

I shook my head. "Sorry. It slipped." I laughed as I stirred the giant pot of sauce. My cell phone rang from my back pocket and I wiped my hands on a dish towel before pulling it out to answer.

"You have dinner covered for a minute?" I asked, and my mother just shooed me away with her hand.

"I miss you," I said as I answered Cass's call.

"We miss you, too. How are you doing?"

I glanced around the kitchen. "Oh, you know. I'm living the rock-and-roll dream." I laughed.

"I want to come see you in a few weeks, if you're feeling up to it?"

"Everyone?" I didn't want to even mention E's name, but I was dying to see him again.

"I can barely hear you," she yelled in my ear.

"Cass? Can you hear me?" I asked as I walked into the living room, hoping for a better signal.

"Sarah, if you can hear me, go outside. Your signal sucks."

I rolled my eyes as I pushed open the front door. "Can you . . ." My voice caught in my throat as I gazed into E's eyes. He smiled that delicious crooked smile, deep dimples settling in his cheeks.

"Have fun, but not too much fun." Cass laughed in my ear and I couldn't help but smile as the line went dead.

"Oh, for God's sake. Kiss him already or I will," Jenny called out from beside us, and I hadn't even noticed she was there.

E's hand slid around my neck as he pulled my face to his, pressing his lips softly against mine. My hands fell onto his chest as his other arm looped around my back and pulled me tight against him.

"You may be an adult, but . . . ," I heard my mother call out from behind me. E and I both began to laugh as he pressed his forehead against mine.

"I didn't think I'd see you again," I whispered.

"You can't get rid of me that easily."

WE ATE DINNER as E told my mother and sister all about the tour that our bands had done together. I was surprised at how little spaghetti was left after we finished. E filled his plate up twice, and after my mother told him that I had cooked it, he took another serving and smiled with each bite.

He helped me clear the table as my mother went to lie

down in her room and Jenny managed to disappear before she had to help. I washed the plates as E took them from me and dried them with a towel.

"I thought the cook wasn't supposed to clean after the meal."

I laughed and shook my head. "I don't mind. It feels good to be *normal* for once."

"It does. I could get used to this. Nice little home, kick-ass spaghetti, and getting to look at you every day." He winked and my heart fluttered.

"Where did you go?" I asked as I scrubbed the same plate over and over. It killed me when he said good-bye to me at the hospital, and what I really wanted to know was if he planned to leave again.

"I had to take care of a few things before I could move forward." He pulled the plate from my hand as his eyes met mine. "I went to see my parents."

"Are you okay?"

"I'm getting there." He grinned and I kissed the dimple on his cheek.

I let the soapy water drain from the sink, and E and I went out front to sit on the porch as the sun began to set. His body was pressed to my side and he took my hand in his, lacing our fingers together as his eyes danced over the healing wounds on my arm.

"I'll never be able to apologize enough for letting you down."

"You didn't let me down and this isn't your fault. It was inevitable that it would all come to a head eventually."

We stared out at the sky as the daylight faded, shooting pink and purple splashes across the clouds.

"If you knew what Derek was doing, why didn't you tell me?" I was scared to look at him as I spoke.

"I couldn't be the one to hurt you, Sarah. It wasn't fair that he put any of us in that position."

I nodded in understanding. I wouldn't have wanted to tell someone that I cared about that his or her relationship was a lie either, but I didn't feel like any less of a fool. That was Derek's fault, not E's.

"Where is Donna?"

His hand squeezed mine as he sighed loudly. "I have no idea."

I pulled my eyebrows together as I studied his profile.

"Donna was never anything more than a friend. It wouldn't have ever worked out between us. She knew my heart was already taken."

"We are a fucked-up bunch."

He laughed deep in his chest. "Maybe that is why we are so perfect for each other."

"Are you going to be here for a while?" I braced for the news that he would be leaving and I would have to deal with life without him again.

"For now I am going to get a room. I saw a trashy little

motel not far from here. I figured tomorrow you could help me find an apartment. Nothing big, just a place to sleep." He yawned loudly at the end of his sentence.

My heart leapt into my throat. He wanted to stay here for the long haul. "I can drive you over there. Jenny will let me use her car. I just have to get the keys." I wasn't ready to say good-bye to him, but I knew he was jet-lagged. I stood up, reluctantly letting his hand go as I went inside to talk to my sister. She was in her room playing around on her laptop as she sprawled out on her stomach across her bed.

"Can I use your car to take E to a hotel? I won't be gone long."

She grinned up at me as she nodded to her purse on her dresser. "I wondered how long it would be until you guys wanted to jump each other. Take it. Just make sure you have it back here by lunch tomorrow. I need to take Mom in to her appointment."

"I was just going to drop him off." I rummaged through her purse for her keys.

"Poor guy. He leaves his band and drops everything and he still can't get any action."

"What do you know about it?"

"We talked." She glanced up from the computer screen and winked.

I put my hands on my hips as I narrowed my eyes at her. "What did he say?"

She shrugged as she clicked the mouse a few times, but I just watched her, waiting for an answer.

"He just said that he understands all you had been through and he doesn't care if you only want to be his friend. He isn't going anywhere. It's kind of romantic." She focused on her screen again as I thought over what she said.

E had given up everything to make sure I was okay, even if it meant he got nothing in return. Derek had never put my feelings before his, and I realized how stupid I had been all along. "Don't wait up."

Jenny smiled again as I left her room, keys in hand. E was still sitting where I had left him, staring up at the now-black sky, dotted with stars.

"You ready?" I asked as I stood behind him, my heart racing at the thought that it was finally just us, no one else.

He turned around to look up at me. "Since the day I met you." He pushed off the side of the porch and stood in the grass, holding out his arms to me. I stepped forward and his hands slid over my hips to my waist as he gripped my sides and lowered me to the ground in front of him. His lips fell on mine softly.

CHAPTER

Forty-Five

ERIC

SARAH HANDED ME the keys and we got into her sister's car and headed toward the hotel. Her guitar was lying over my bags on the backseat and she smiled when she saw it.

"I thought that was gone forever." She reached behind her and ran her fingers over the strings.

I grabbed her hand and pulled it to my lips to kiss it. "I want to hear you sing again."

We pulled into the hotel and Sarah surprised me when she got out of the car and grabbed her guitar from the backseat. I grabbed my bags and slung them over my shoulder.

"You coming in?" I asked as I rounded the car to her side.

"You said you wanted to hear me sing."

I grabbed her free hand and pulled her toward the office. An older woman sat at the desk and eyed us suspiciously. "We don't rent by the hour. This isn't that type of establishment."

I couldn't help but chuckle, but Sarah looked livid. "No. The room is for me. I need something for a few days."

The woman thought it over before she typed away on her keyboard and looked back to me. "I have something available. It is fifty-three dollars and ninety-nine cents a night. How many nights would you like?"

"Let's start with two."

I handed the woman my bank card, and after what felt like an eternity she handed me the key to my room. We made our way to the opposite end of the building and up a flight of stairs outside.

The room was small but it had a bed and a minifridge with a microwave on top. That is all I needed. I knew I would be spending most of my spare time with Sarah anyway. I just needed a place to lay my head. I turned on the light and it flickered as Sarah stepped inside and closed the door behind her.

"It will do," I said as I slid my bag off my shoulder.

Sarah raised an eyebrow at me as she struggled not to laugh. "We will find you an apartment tomorrow."

I turned to her, placing a hand on either side of her face as I pulled her mouth to mine. She pressed her body against me as her hands slid up to the back of my neck and into my hair. I ran my tongue over her lower lip and she let her lips part, inviting me to kiss her the way I had dreamed about since the first day I saw her.

She moaned quietly into my mouth and I turned us so her back was against the door. I didn't want to push her after all I knew about her past. I couldn't stand it if I hurt her again, but she didn't resist and her tongue slid over mine and our kisses became hungrier.

I pulled my mouth from hers to search her eyes. "Is this okay?"

She nodded as she stared up at me through hooded eyes.

"I love you," I whispered, my lips moving against hers. Finally saying those words was terrifying and liberating.

"I love you, too," she said back just as quietly.

My heart raced as my hands slid down to her hips and pulled her toward me. "Say it again." I kissed her lips and she giggled.

"I love you."

I growled as I lifted her, and her legs wrapped around my hips. "Again."

"I love you."

Her forehead was against mine as I carried her to the small bed in the center of the room and lowered her onto the mattress. I hovered over her as I stared into her eyes. I grabbed her wrists and slowly pulled her arm toward my mouth, placing a kiss on the jagged scars that marred her perfect porcelain skin. "Maybe we can help each other heal."

"I'd like that." A tear fell from her eye to the blanket below. She reached between us and gripped the bottom of my shirt, tugging it toward my head. I grabbed it and yanked it over my head as she pushed up from the bed and placed a kiss on my chest above my heart. "You keep your scars on the inside." She ran her fingers over the spot her lips had just touched as my heart raced. I lowered myself on top of her, needing to be as close as possible. Her mouth pressed against mine and the urgency was gone. Neither of us was running away again. It was only us and we would work on healing each other. I didn't care if it took months or years.

I ran my hand down her side and gripped her hip as I trailed kissed over her jaw and down the hollow of her throat. Her head fell to the side as my mouth slid over her shoulder. I lifted off her and grabbed the bottom of her shirt, tugging it up. She lifted her arms so I could pull it easily over her head, and I stared down at her beautiful body. I relaxed back against her, continuing my trail of kisses down to place one over her heart as I slid her bra strap from her shoulder. My eyes met hers briefly to make sure she didn't object.

I couldn't count the number of women I had been with in my lifetime, but I had never once made love. My hands slid behind her back as she arched from the bed so I could unclasp her bra. I tugged it down her arms as my mouth dipped lower, kissing her breast as her hands slid down over my back and her fingernails dug into my flesh. I ran my tongue over the tattoo on her ribs that read COURAGE in cursive.

I trailed kisses down her stomach, worshipping every inch of her flesh. I ran my fingers along the edge of her jeans so lightly it tickled her and she squirmed. "Are you sure about this?"

"I've never been more sure about anything."

I slid my finger behind the button of her jeans and popped it free before sliding down her zipper. She lifted her hips from the bed as I tugged the jeans down her legs and tossed them on the floor. I pushed to my feet as she stared up at me and undid my jeans, then I kicked them off next to hers. She crawled back to the center of the bed and I climbed over her, my mouth finding hers again as I tangled my fingers in her hair.

CHAPTER Forty-Six

SARAH

EVERY NERVE ENDING in my body was on fire. I was terrified but never wanted anything else more in my life than I wanted E. He was treating me as if I were going to break under his touch and I struggled not to take things too fast.

Everything up to this moment melted away as his tongue slid over mine. My hands trailed down over the muscles in his back, each pulling and flexing under my touch until I reached the elastic band of his boxers. I slid them lower as I grabbed his ass and he laughed against my mouth.

His weight rested on one arm beside my head as his fingers ran over my ribs, causing me to shiver. He slipped his fingers in the side of my navy-blue panties and tugged them down a few inches.

I could feel how badly he wanted me as his hips pushed against mine, only a few layers of thin fabric keeping us from finally being together. He groaned as I pushed my hips against him, and his teeth bit lightly into my bottom lip as he tugged at it gently. I used my other hand to push down the other side of his boxers as his hand slid over my bottom, shoving my panties down farther.

He left fire in the wake of his touch and it was driving me insane. I rolled my tongue over his upper lip as our breathing accelerated and our bodies became hungrier for each other.

"Say it again," he half moaned as he tugged at the thin fabric of my panties and it bit into my skin.

"I love you," I panted, and I heard the material rip, and now only one article of clothing stood between us. His hand slid up over my ribs and he cupped my breast, sliding his thumb over my nipple and causing it to peak under his touch.

"I love you so much," he growled as his mouth continued to move against mine and his hips pushed against me again. I moved against him, desperate for the release that was building inside me.

My hand pushed against his boxers but could not reach low enough to remove them. My nails dug into his hips and he laughed as he reached down and shoved the boxers lower, then kicked them off. His warm, hard body was back against mine in an instant. I struggled to control my breathing as he pressed against my entrance. I wrapped my legs around his waist as my arms looped around his neck to hold his body against mine.

He rocked gently against me and he was much larger than I expected, but my body was more than ready for him. He took his time as he slowly entered me, his eyes looking into mine until he had filled me completely. His hips stilled as he allowed my body to adjust to him as his forehead rested against mine and our breaths mingled.

I slowly rolled my hips and he began to move against me. I had never before felt like this in my life. I had no idea that being with someone could ever feel this way. Soon our bodies were covered in a thin layer of sweat as our skin slid against each other in perfect rhythm as if we were made for each other.

E's free hand was tangled in my hair and he was careful not to rest all his weight on me. I had done the act so many times before, but this was something new, something I didn't even know was possible, and I felt as if I were finally feeling for the first time in my life. I loved him with every fiber of my being. My body and my heart had known it all along.

His hips began to move more urgently and I rolled mine against his, eliciting a delicious groan from the back of his throat that rumbled from his chest.

The tightening in my belly slowly rolled lower, and I could feel it all the way to my toes as I fell over the edge of pleasure. E kept perfect rhythm with me until my body relaxed beneath him and he let go himself, his muscles tightening and relaxing under my hands until he moaned against my lips and his full weight pressed against me.

He kissed me softly on the lips, his fingers tightening in my hair before he rolled over beside me and pulled me into his arms.

"I don't ever want to let you go." He pressed his lips against my hair.

I closed my eyes, exhausted and satisfied. "I won't let you," I whispered as I closed my eyes and let exhaustion take over.

I loved sleeping with his arms around me, and for the first time in as long as I could remember, I didn't have a nightmare about my childhood. E slept soundly, too, and by the time morning came, I wanted to force myself to sleep longer.

"How are you feeling?" he asked as he pressed a kiss to my temple from behind me.

"Happy." I stretched, arching my back, and he groaned as I pushed against him.

"I am, too, and you are making me even happier as you do that." He laughed, his chest vibrating against my back as his arms held me tighter.

I was terrified all of this new happiness would be ripped away. "What now?"

"Now?" He pushed up on his elbow. "We take it one day at a time."

I slid onto my back so I could look up at him, and he leaned over me, pressing his lips against mine.

"Are you really going to get an apartment here?" I slid my fingers through his messy hair.

"Unless you would rather keep meeting in a seedy hotel?" He cocked his eyebrow.

"It is kind of romantic in a just-killed-someone-and-hid-their-body-in-the-closet kind of way," I joked.

"I promise to tell you about each skeleton in my closet if you tell me yours."

"Deal." I pressed my lips against his and his hand slid over my stomach and it growled. We both laughed as he rolled onto his back beside me.

"I guess we could start the day with some food." He glanced over at me and I nodded reluctantly. I was more than happy to spend the day in bed with him, but Jenny needed her car and we needed to find a better place for E to stay. And we had from now until forever to make love to each other.

Epilogue

ERIC

I T HAD BEEN three months since I'd showed up on Sarah's door-step. We knew that if we ever wanted to have a fighting chance, we would need to take things slowly, even though it felt as if I had waited my entire life for her.

I got an apartment a few blocks away from her, and we hung out as much as possible. We saw every movie that came out in the-aters and wrote music together. We finally finished our song and had moved on to writing an entire album of our own because our story was far from over.

She continued to go to therapy twice a week and I began to go as well. I didn't want to be the reason that we didn't make it. As much as I hated reliving my past, I loved Sarah more.

I completed my community service while Sarah spent time with her family. I even called my mother about once a week just to let her know how my life was going. I hoped one day we would be able to be close the way Sarah had become with her family, but it would take some time.

The new Damaged tour began and we were on the road again, but this time I had Sarah at my side. It was great to see her and Cass together again.

The tour kicked off with a concert in Arizona. Sarah was a nervous wreck. She was the opening act for us this time around and it would be only her onstage. We went over every lyric of the songs we had written until she finally started to relax.

I wouldn't have pushed her to perform, but I knew that she needed to get back onstage. It would help her move forward and it was what she was born to do.

The crowd was huge and our new manager, Dave, was barking orders at us as he paced the floor backstage.

"You need to calm the hell down." Chris threw his guitar pick at Dave and he ducked as we all laughed.

"At least we don't have to worry about E sleeping with him." Tucker's eyes met mine with a smirk.

"Fuck you." I shook my head, thankful Cass and Sarah were off getting ready for the night.

"LESS IS MORE," Cass said as she took my eyeliner from my hand.

"I'm not ready to do this." I chewed on my lip as I inspected my face in the mirror.

"You were born ready. E will be right with you the whole time."

I smoothed my hands down over my gray dress, which stopped midthigh. I watched her eyes dance over the bandage on my arm.

"I guess I need to take this off, huh?" I asked, and she nodded. I slowly pulled back the medical tape from the bandage that covered my forearm.

"That looks amazing," Cass said, looking over the sparrows that now covered my ROCK TATTOO.

"Thank you." I rubbed my fingers over the raised lines from the fresh ink. One bird for E and one for me. It was us finally breaking free from the cages of our pasts. I smiled as I thought about how far we had come in the last few months.

I didn't know where we would be tomorrow, but we just focused on the here and now, and slowly we grew stronger.

"You ready?" Cass asked as she cocked her head to the side as her hand absentmindedly rubbed over her growing belly.

I placed my hand over her stomach and smiled at her proudly. "Aunt Sarah is going to make you proud, little rock star."

She smiled back at me, her face glowing. I walked down the hall toward E and the guys, and Cass followed me. As we walked into the room, I felt that I was home.

I knew I would always have my mother and sister, but my family had grown; it just took me a while to realize it.

"Don't even say it, Tucker." Cass waved her hand as she walked over to him and sat on his lap. He grunted as if she weighed a ton and she smacked him playfully on the chest. "I'm going out there to see your first concert of the tour. Sarah needs me."

His hand covered her belly as he gave her a kiss on the nose. "It's too loud."

She rolled her eyes as I walked over to E and slid against his side, his arms wrapping around me as he laughed at Tucker.

"This is the end of rock and roll," Terry grumbled as he shook his head. "Next he will have us playing lullabies."

"You won't be playing at all if I find out you are still texting my little sister." I narrowed my eyes at Terry and he barked out a laugh.

"Showtime, guys. Let's make history," Dave, the new manager, called over the laughter as he pulled open the door to the room. We all stood and filed out of the cramped space toward the stage.

The excitement was palpable, and as scary as it was, we couldn't wait to see what the future held for all of us.

The twins, Tucker, and Cass all lined up beside the stage, hidden behind the curtain as E and I made our way out in front of the crowd. I looked over at him, butterflies taking flight in my belly as my fingers wrapped around the microphone. He winked and mouthed, *I love you*, as he began to strum his guitar. The opening notes to the first song we had written together filled the arena.

As soon as I began to sing, the fear left me and all I could feel was the love of the man who sat to my left. Each song blended into the next until it was over, and the crowd cheered for us as E pulled me against his chest and kissed me proudly. I had tears in my eyes as I took the guitar from him and left the stage.

Damaged took the stage as E made himself at home behind his drums. Cass and I watched proudly as they played to cheers and screams from all of their devoted fans. We had been through a lot as a group, and this moment made it all worth it. The struggle and the fighting to overcome our demons all washed away as the world accepted us for who we were.

As the band played their final song, Cass began to cry as the crowd sang along to the words she had written. I looped my arm over her shoulders and we gently swayed along as Tucker sang, a proud smile on his face as he looked over at his pregnant wife.

"Thank you all so much for coming out and supporting us. It has been a long road to get here, but we are excited to continue down it and see where it leads." The room went wild with support, and Tucker waited for the noise to die down before he continued. "If you don't mind, we'd like to play one more song for you."

The twins began to play, and now it was my turn to cry as "Free Bird" filled the air. Tucker smiled as he motioned with his hand for us to join him onstage. I gripped Cass's hand in mine tightly as we walked onstage. Tucker took a step back from the mic as he wrapped his arm around his wife and pressed a kiss to her temple. I stared out at the sea of people, all supportive and cheering me on as I started to sing with tears streaming down my face.

Everyone sang along with me—the crowd, the band. My voice grew from shaky to confident as I gave everything I had to give to them. I glanced over my shoulder at E, who smiled as he sang along, knowing what the song meant to me. I fell impossibly deeper in love with him in that moment.

I poured my soul into every word as I let that part of my life go, accepting the unknown and ready to take on whatever life held for me with E by my side. I was finally free as a bird.

Acknowledgments

ENORMOUS THANK YOU to everyone at Gallery, Trident, and all the others who work behind the scenes to make these books possible.